THE OVERCOAT
AND
THE NOSE

NIKOLAI GOGOL

THE OVERCOAT
AND
THE NOSE

Translated by
Ronald Wilks

penguin books

PENGUIN BOOKS
Published by the Penguin Group
Penguin Books USA Inc., 375 Hudson Street,
New York, New York 10014, U.S.A.
Penguin Books Ltd, 27 Wrights Lane,
London W8 5TZ, England
Penguin Books Australia Ltd, Ringwood,
Victoria, Australia
Penguin Books Canada Ltd, 10 Alcorn Avenue,
Toronto, Ontario, Canada M4V 3B2
Penguin Books (N.Z.) Ltd, 182–190 Wairau Road,
Auckland 10, New Zealand

Penguin Books Ltd, Registered Offices:
Harmondsworth, Middlesex, England

Published in Penguin Books 1995

This translation of "The Overcoat" and "The Nose" appears in *Diary
of a Madman and Other Stories* by Nikolai Gogol, translated by Ronald
Wilks, published by Penguin Books.

ISBN 0 14 60.0114 1

Printed in the United States of America

CONTENTS

The Overcoat

In one of our government departments . . . but perhaps I had better not say exactly *which* one. For no one's more touchy than people in government departments, regiments, chancelleries or indeed *any* kind of official body. Nowadays every private citizen thinks the whole of society is insulted when he himself is. They say that not so long ago a complaint was lodged by a District Police Inspector (I cannot remember which town he came from) and in this he made it quite plain that the State and all its laws were going to rack and ruin, and that his own holy name had been taken in vain without any shadow of doubt. To substantiate his claim he appended as supplementary evidence an absolutely enormous tome, containing a highly romantic composition, in which nearly every ten pages a police commissioner made an appearance, sometimes in a very drunken state. And so, to avoid any *further* unpleasantness, we had better call the department in question *a certain department*.

In a certain department, then, there worked *a certain civil servant*. On no account could he be said to have a memorable appearance; he was shortish, rather pock-marked, with reddish hair, and also had weak eyesight, or so it seemed. He

1

had a small bald patch in front and both cheeks were wrinkled. His complexion was the sort you find in those who suffer from piles ... but there's nothing anyone can do about that: the Petersburg climate is to blame.

As for his rank in the civil service (this must be determined before we go any further) he belonged to the species known as perpetual titular councillor, for far too long now, as we all know, mocked and jeered by certain writers with the very commendable habit of attacking those who are in no position to retaliate. His surname was Bashmachkin, which all too plainly was at some time derived from *bashmak*.

But exactly when and what time of day and how the name originated is a complete mystery. Both his father and his grandfather, and even his brother-in-law and all the other Bashmachkins went around in boots and had them soled only three times a year. His name was Akaky Akakievich. This may appear an odd name to our reader and somewhat far-fetched, but we can assure him that no one went out of his way to find it, and that the way things turned out he just could not have been called *anything* else. This is how it all happened: Akaky Akakievich was born on the night of 22 March, if my memory serves me right. His late mother, the wife of a civil servant and a very fine woman, made all the necessary arrangements for the christening. At the time she was still lying in her bed, facing the door, and on her right stood the godfather, Ivan Ivanovich Yeroshkin, a most excellent gentleman who was a chief clerk in the Senate, and the godmother, Arina Semyonovna Belobrushkova, the wife of a district police inspector and a woman of the rarest virtue. The mother was offered a choice of three names: Mokkia, Sossia, or Khozdazat, after the martyr. 'Oh no,' his mother thought, 'such awful names they're going in for these days!' To try and please her they turned over a few pages in the calendar and again three peculiar names popped up: Triphily, Dula and Varakhasy. 'It's sheer punishment sent from above!' the woman muttered. 'What names! For the life of me, I've never seen anything like them. Varadat or Varukh wouldn't be so bad but as for Triphily and Varakhasy!' They turned over yet another page and found Pavsikakhy and Vakhtisy. 'Well, it's plain enough that this is fate. So we'd better call him after his father. He was an Akaky, so let's call his son Akaky as well.' And that was how he became Akaky Akakievich. The child was christened and during the ceremony he burst into tears and made such a face it was plain that he knew there and then that he was fated to be a titular councillor. The reason for all this narrative is to enable our reader to judge for himself that the whole train of events was absolutely predetermined and that for Akaky to have any other name was quite impossible.

Exactly *when* he entered the department, and who was responsible for the appointment, no one can say for sure. No matter how many directors and principals came and went, he was always to be seen in precisely the same place, sitting in exactly the same position, doing exactly the same work—just routine copying, pure and simple. Subsequently everyone came to believe that he had come into this world already equipped for his job, complete with uniform and bald patch. No one showed him the least respect in the office. The porters not only remained seated when he went by, but they did not so much as give him a look—as though a common housefly had just flown across the waiting-room. Some assistant to the head clerk would shove some papers right under his nose, without even so much as saying: 'Please copy this out', or 'Here's an interesting little job', or some pleasant remark you might expect to hear in refined establishments. He would take whatever was put in front of him without looking up to see who had put it there or questioning whether he had any right to do so, his eyes fixed only on his work. He would simply take the documents and immediately start copying them out. The junior clerks laughed and told jokes at his expense—as far as office wit would stretch—telling stories they had made up themselves, even while they were standing right next to him, about his seventy-year-old landlady, for example, who used to beat him, or so they said. They would ask when the wedding was going to be and shower his head with little bits of paper, calling them snow.

But Akaky Akakievich did not make the slightest protest, just as though there were nobody there at all. His work was not even affected and he never copied out one wrong letter in the face of all this annoyance. Only if the jokes became too unbearable—when somebody jogged his elbow, for example, and stopped him from working—would he say: 'Leave me alone, why do you have to torment me?' There was something strange in these words and the way he said them. His voice had a peculiar sound which made you feel sorry for him, so much so that one clerk who was new to the department, and who was about to follow the example of the others and have a good laugh at him, suddenly stopped dead in his tracks, as though transfixed, and from that time onwards saw everything in a different light. Some kind of supernatural power alienated him from his colleagues whom, on first acquaintance, he had taken to be respectable, civilized men. And for a long time afterwards, even during his gayest moments, he would see that stooping figure with a bald patch in front, muttering pathetically: 'Leave me alone, why do you have to torment me?' And in these piercing words he could hear the sound of others: 'I am your brother.' The poor young man would bury his face in his hands and many times later in life shuddered at the thought of how brutal men could be and how the most refined manners and breeding often concealed the most savage coarseness, even, dear God, in someone universally recognized for his honesty and uprightness . . .

One would be hard put to find a man anywhere who so lived for his work. To say he worked with zeal would be an understatement: no, he worked *with love*. In that copying of his he glimpsed a whole varied and pleasant world of his own. One could see the enjoyment on his face. Some letters were his favourites, and whenever he came to write them out he would be beside himself with excitement, softly laughing to himself and winking, willing his pen on with his lips, so you could tell what letter his pen was carefully tracing just by looking at him. Had his rewards been at all commensurate with his enthusiasm, he might perhaps have been promoted to state councillor, much to his own surprise. But as the wags in the office put it, all he got for his labour was a badge in his button-hole and piles on his backside. However, you could not say he was *completely* ignored. One of the directors, a kindly gentleman, who wished to reward him for his long service, once ordered him to be given something rather more important than ordinary copying—the preparation of a report for another department from a completed file. All this entailed was altering the title page and changing a few verbs from the first to the third person. This caused him so much trouble that he broke out in a sweat, kept mopping his brow, and finally said: 'No, you'd better let me stick to plain copying.' After that they left him to go on copying for ever and ever. Apart from this copying nothing else existed as far as he was concerned. He gave no thought at all to his clothes: his uniform was not what you might call green, but a mealy white tinged with red.

His collar was very short and narrow, so that his neck, which could not exactly be called long, appeared to stick out for miles, like those plaster kittens with wagging heads foreign street-pedlars carry around by the dozen. Something was always sure to be sticking to his uniform—a wisp of straw or piece of thread. What is more, he had the strange knack of passing underneath windows just as some rubbish was being emptied and this explained why he was perpetually carrying around scraps of melon rind and similar refuse on his hat. Not once in his life did he notice what was going on in the street he passed down every day, unlike his young colleagues in the Service, who are famous for their hawk-like eyes—eyes so sharp that they can even see whose trouser-strap has come undone on the other side of the pavement, something which never fails to bring a sly grin to their faces. But even if Akaky Akakievich did happen to notice something, all he ever saw were rows of letters in his own neat, regular handwriting.

Only if a horse's muzzle appeared from out of nowhere, propped itself on his shoulder and fanned his cheek with a gust from its nostrils—only then did he realize he was not in the middle of a sentence but in the middle of the street. As soon as he got home he would sit down at the table, quickly swallow his cabbage soup, and eat some beef and onions, tasting absolutely nothing and gulping everything down, together with whatever the Good Lord happened to provide at the time, flies included. When he saw that his stomach was beginning to swell he would get up from the table, fetch his inkwell and start copying out documents he had brought home with him. If he had no work from the office, he would copy out something else, just for his own personal pleasure—

7

especially if the document in question happened to be re-markable not for its stylistic beauty, but because it was addressed to some newly appointed or important person.

Even at that time of day when the light has completely faded from the grey St Petersburg sky and the whole clerical brotherhood has eaten its fill, according to salary and palate; when everyone has rested from departmental pen-pushing and running around; when his own and everyone else's absolutely indispensable labours have been forgotten—as well as all those other things that restless man sets himself to do of his own free will—sometimes even more than is really necessary; when the civil servant dashes off to enjoy his remaining hours of freedom as much as he can (one showing a more daring spirit by careering off to the theatre; another sauntering down the street to spend his time looking at cheap little hats in the shop windows; another going off to a party to waste his time flattering a pretty girl, the shining light of some small circle of civil servants; while another—and this happens more often than not—goes off to visit a friend from the office living on the third or second floor, in two small rooms with hall and kitchen, and with some pretensions to fashion in the form of a lamp or some little trifle which has cost a great many sacrifices, refusals to invitations to dinner or country outings); in short, at that time of day when all the civil servants have dispersed to their friends' little flats for a game of whist, sipping tea from glasses and nibbling little biscuits, drawing on their long pipes, and giving an account while dealing out the cards of the latest scandal which has wafted down from high society—a Russian can *never* resist stories; or when there is nothing new to talk about, bringing out once again the old anecdote about the Commandant who was told that the tail of the horse in Falconet's statue of Peter the Great had been cut off; briefly, when everyone was doing his best to amuse himself, Akaky Akakievich did not abandon himself to any such pleasures.

No one could remember ever having seen him at a party. After he had copied to his heart's content he would go to bed, smiling in anticipation of the next day and what God would send him to copy. So passed the uneventful life of a man quite content with his four hundred roubles a year; and this life might have continued to pass peacefully until ripe old age had it not been for the various calamities that lie in wait not only for titular councillors, but even privy, state, court and all types of councillor, even those who give advice to no one, nor take it from anyone.

St Petersburg harbours one terrible enemy of all those earning four hundred roubles a year—or thereabouts. This enemy is nothing else than our northern frost, although some people say it is very good for the health. Between eight and nine in the morning, just when the streets are crowded with civil servants on their way to the office, it starts dealing out indiscriminately such sharp nips to noses of every description that the poor clerks just do not know where to put them. At this time of day, when the foreheads of even important officials ache from the frost and tears well up in their eyes, the humbler titular councillors are sometimes quite defenceless. Their only salvation lies in running the length of five or six streets in their thin, wretched little overcoats and then having a really good stamp in the lobby until their faculties and capacity for office work have thawed out. For some time now Akaky Akakievich had been feeling that his back and shoulders had become subject to really vicious onslaughts no matter how fast he tried to sprint the official distance between home and office. At length he began to wonder if his overcoat might not be at fault here.

After giving it a thorough examination at home he found that in two or three places—to be exact, on the back and round the shoulders—it now resembled coarse cheese-cloth: the material had worn so thin that it was almost transparent and the lining had fallen to pieces.

At this point it should be mentioned that Akaky Akakievich's coat was a standing joke in the office. It had been deprived of the status of overcoat and was called a dressing-gown instead. And there was really something very strange in the way it was made. With the passing of the years the collar had shrunk more and more, as the cloth from it had been used to patch up other parts. This repair work showed no sign of a tailor's hand, and made the coat look baggy and most unsightly. When he realized what was wrong, Akaky Akakievich decided he would have to take the overcoat to Petrovich, a tailor living somewhere on the third floor up some backstairs and who, in spite of being blind in one eye and having pockmarks all over his face, carried on quite a nice little business repairing civil servants' and other gentlemen's trousers and frock-coats, whenever—it goes without saying—he was sober and was not hatching some plot in that head of his.

Of course, there is not much point in wasting our time describing this tailor, but since it has become the accepted thing to give full details about every single character in a story, there is nothing for it but to take a look at this man Petrovich.

At first he was simply called Grigory and had been a serf belonging to some gentleman or other. People started calling him Petrovich after he had gained his freedom, from which time he began to drink rather heavily on every church holiday—at first only on the most important feast-days, but later on every single holiday marked by a cross in the calendar. In this respect he was faithful to ancestral tradition, and when he had rows about this with his wife he called her a worldly woman and a German.

As we have now brought his wife up we might as well say something about her. Unfortunately, little is known of her except that she was Petrovich's wife and she wore a bonnet instead of a shawl. Apparently she had nothing to boast about as far as looks were concerned. At least only *guardsmen* were ever known to peep under her bonnet as they tweaked their moustaches and made a curious noise in their throats.

As he made his way up the stairs to Petrovich's (these stairs, to describe them accurately, were running with water and slops, and were saturated with that strong smell of spirit which makes the eyes smart and is a perpetual feature of all backstairs in Petersburg), Akaky Akakievich was already beginning to wonder how much Petrovich would charge and making up his mind not to pay more than two roubles. The door had been left open as his wife had been frying some kind of fish and had made so much smoke in the kitchen that not even the cockroaches were visible.

Mrs Petrovich herself failed to notice Akaky Akakievich as he walked through the kitchen and finally entered a room where Petrovich was squatting on a broad, bare wooden table, his feet crossed under him like a Turkish Pasha. As is customary with tailors, he was working in bare feet. The first thing that struck Akaky was his familiar big toe with its deformed nail, thick and hard as tortoiseshell. A skein of silk and some thread hung round his neck and some old rags lay across his lap. For the past two or three minutes he had been trying to thread a needle without any success, which made him curse the poor light and even the thread itself. He grumbled under his breath: 'Why don't you go through, you swine! You'll be the death of me, you devil!'

Akaky Akakievich was not very pleased at finding Petrovich in such a temper: his real intention had been to place an order with Petrovich after he had been on the bottle, or, as his wife put it, 'after he'd bin swigging that corn brandy again, the old one-eyed devil!'

In this state Petrovich would normally be very amenable, invariably agreeing to any price quite willingly and even concluding the deal by bowing and saying thank you. It is true that afterwards his tearful wife would come in with the same sad story that that husband of hers was drunk again and had not charged enough. But even so, for another kopeck or two the deal was usually settled. But at this moment Petrovich was (or so it seemed) quite sober, and as a result was gruff, intractable and in the right mood for charging the devil's own price. Realizing this, Akaky Akakievich was all for making himself scarce, as the saying goes, but by then it was too late. Petrovich had already screwed up his one eye and was squinting steadily at him. Akaky Akakievich found himself saying:

'Good morning, Petrovich!'

'Good morning to you, sir,' said Petrovich, staring at Akaky's hand to see how much money he had on him.

'I . . . er . . . came about that . . . Petrovich.'

The reader should know that Akaky Akakievich spoke mainly in prepositions, adverbs, and resorted to parts of speech which had no meaning whatsoever. If the subject was particularly complicated he would even leave whole sentences unfinished, so that very often he would begin with: 'That is really exactly what . . .' and then forget to say anything more, convinced that he had said what he wanted to.

13

'What on earth's that?' Petrovich said, inspecting with his solitary eye every part of Akaky's uniform, beginning with the collar and sleeves, then the back, tails and buttonholes. All of this was very familiar territory, as it was his own work, but every tailor usually carries out this sort of inspection when he has a customer.

'I've er . . . come . . . Petrovich, that overcoat you know, the cloth . . . you see, it's quite strong in other places, only a little dusty. This makes it look old, but in fact it's quite new. Just a bit . . . you know . . . on the back and a little worn on one shoulder, and a bit . . . you know, on the other, that's all. Only a small job . . .'

Petrovich took the 'dressing-gown', laid it out on the table, took a long look at it, shook his head, reached out to the window-sill for his round snuff-box bearing the portrait of some general—exactly which one is hard to say, as someone had poked his finger through the place where his face should have been and it was pasted over with a square piece of paper.

Petrovich took a pinch of snuff, held the coat up to the light, gave it another thorough scrutiny and shook his head again. Then he placed it with the lining upwards, shook his head once more, removed the snuff-box lid with the pasted-over general, filled his nose with snuff, replaced the lid, put the box away somewhere, and finally said: 'No, I can't mend that. It's in a *terrible* state!'

With these words Akaky Akakievich's heart sank.

'And why not, Petrovich?' he asked in the imploring voice of a child. 'It's only a bit worn on the shoulders. Really, you could *easily* patch it up.'

'I've got plenty of patches, plenty,' said Petrovich, 'But I can't sew them all up together. The coat's absolutely rotten. It'll fall to pieces if you so much as touch it with a needle.'

'Well, if it falls to bits you can patch it up again.'

'But it's too far gone. There's nothing for the patches to hold on to. You can hardly call it cloth at all. One gust of wind and the whole lot will blow away.'

'But patch it up just a *little*. It can't, hm, be, well . . .'

'I'm afraid it can't be done, sir,' replied Petrovich firmly. 'It's too far gone. You'd be better off if you cut it up for the winter and made some leggings with it, because socks aren't any good in the really cold weather. The Germans invented them as they thought they could make money out of them.' (Petrovich liked to have a dig at Germans.) 'As for the coat, you'll have to have a *new* one, sir.'

The word 'new' made Akaky's eyes cloud over and everything in the room began to swim round. All he could see clearly was the pasted-over face of the general on Petrovich's snuff-box.

'What do you mean, a *new* one?' he said as though in a dream. 'I've got no money.'

'Yes, you'll have to have a new one,' Petrovich said in a cruelly detached voice.

'Well, um, if I had a *new* one, how would, I mean to say, er . . . ?'

'You mean, how much?'

'Yes.'

'You can reckon on three fifty-rouble notes or more,' said Petrovich pressing his lips together dramatically. He had a great liking for strong dramatic effects, and loved producing some remark intended to shock and then watching the expression on the other person's face out of the corner of his eye.

'A hundred and fifty roubles for an overcoat!' poor Akaky shrieked for what was perhaps the first time in his life—he was well known for his low voice.

'Yes, sir,' said Petrovich. 'And even then it wouldn't be much to write home about. If you want a collar made from marten fur and a silk-lined hood then it could set you back as much as two hundred.'

'Petrovich, please,' said Akaky imploringly, not hearing, or at least, trying not to hear Petrovich's 'dramatic' pronouncement, 'just do what you can with it, so I can wear it a little longer.'

'I'm afraid it's no good. It would be sheer waste of time and money,' Petrovich added, and with these words Akaky left, feeling absolutely crushed.

After he had gone Petrovich stayed squatting where he was for some time without continuing his work, his lips pressed together significantly. He felt pleased he had not cheapened himself or the rest of the sartorial profession.

Out in the street Akaky felt as if he were in a dream. 'What a to-do now,' he said to himself. 'I never thought it would turn out like this, for the life of me . . .' And then, after a brief silence, he added: 'Well now then! So this is how it's turned out and I would never have guessed it would end . . .' Whereupon followed a long silence, after which he murmured: 'So that's it! Really, to tell the truth, it's so unexpected that I never would have . . . such a to-do!' When he had said this, instead of going home, he walked straight off in the opposite direction, quite oblivious of what he was doing. On the way a chimney-sweeper brushed up against him and made his shoulder black all over. And then a whole hatful of lime fell on him from the top of a house that was being built. To this he was blind as well; and only when he happened to bump into a policeman who had propped his halberd up and was sprinkling some snuff he had taken from a small horn on to his wart-covered fist did he come to his senses at all, and only then because the policeman said:

'Isn't the pavement wide enough without you having to crawl right up my nose?'

This brought Akaky to his senses and he went off in the direction of home.

Not until he was there did he begin to collect his thoughts and properly assess the situation. He started talking to himself, not in incoherent phrases, but quite rationally and openly, as though he were discussing what had happened with a sensible friend in whom one could confide when it came to matters of the greatest intimacy.

'No, I can see it's impossible to talk to Petrovich now. He's a bit . . . and it looks as if his wife's been knocking him around. I'd better wait until Sunday morning: after he's slept off Saturday night he'll start his squinting again and will be dying for a drink to see him through his hangover. But his wife won't give him any money, so I'll turn up with a kopeck or two. That will soften him up, you know, and my over-coat . . .'

Akaky Akakievich felt greatly comforted by this fine piece of reasoning, and waiting until Sunday came went straight off to Petrovich's. He spotted his wife leaving the house some distance away. Just as he had expected, after Saturday night, Petrovich's eye really was squinting for all it was worth, and there he was, his head drooping towards the floor, and look-ing very sleepy. All the same, as soon as he realized why Akaky had come, he became wide awake, just as though the devil had given him a sharp kick.

'It's impossible, you'll have to have a new one.' At this point Akaky Akakievich shoved a ten-kopeck piece into his hand.

'Much obliged, sir. I'll have a quick pick-me-up on you,' said Petrovich. 'And I shouldn't worry about that overcoat of yours if I were you. It's no good at all. I'll make you a *mar-vellous* new one, so let's leave it at that.'

Akaky Akakievich tried to say something about having it repaired, but Petrovich pretended not to hear and said:

'Don't worry, I'll make you a brand-new one, you can depend on me to make a good job of it. And I might even get some silver clasps for the collar, like they're all wearing now.'

Now Akaky Akakievich realized he would *have* to buy a new overcoat and his heart sank. Where was the money coming from? Of course he could just about count on that holiday bonus. But this had been put aside for something else a long time ago. He needed new trousers, and then there was that long-standing debt to be settled with the shoemaker for putting some new tops on his old boots. And there were three shirts he had to order from the seamstress, as well as two items of underwear which cannot decently be mentioned in print. To cut a long story short, all his money was bespoken and he would not have enough even if the Director were so generous as to raise his bonus to forty-five or even fifty roubles. What was left was pure chicken-feed; in terms of *overcoat* finance, the merest drop in the ocean. Also, he knew very well that at times Petrovich would suddenly take it into his head to charge the most fantastic price, so that even his wife could not help saying about him:

'Has he gone out of his mind, the old fool! One day he'll work for next to nothing, and now the devil's making him charge more than he's worth himself!'

He knew very well, however, that Petrovich would take eighty roubles; but the question still remained, where was he

to get them from? He could just about scrape half of it together, perhaps a little more. But what about the balance?
Before we go into this, the reader should know where the
first half was coming from.

For every rouble he spent, Akaky Akakievich would put
half a kopeck away in a small box, which had a little slot in
the lid for dropping money through, and which was kept
locked. Every six months he would tot up his savings and
change them into silver. He had been doing this for a long
time, and over several years had amassed more than forty
roubles. So, he had half the money, but what about the rest?

Akaky Akakievich thought and thought, and at last decided he would have to cut down on this day-to-day spending, for a year at least: he would have to stop drinking tea in
the evenings; go without a candle; and, if he had copying to
do, go to his landlady's room and work there. He would have
to step as carefully and lightly as possible over the cobbles in
the street—almost on tiptoe—to save the soles of his shoes;
avoid taking his personal linen to the laundress as much as
possible; and, to make his underclothes last longer, take them
off when he got home and only wear his thick cotton
dressing-gown—itself an ancient garment and one which
time had treated kindly. Frankly, Akaky Akakievich found
these privations quite a burden to begin with, but after a
while he got used to them. He even trained himself to go
without any food at all in the evenings, for his nourishment
was *spiritual*, his thoughts always full of that overcoat which

one day was to be his. From that time onwards his whole life seemed to have become richer, as though he had married and another human being was by his side. It was as if he was not alone at all but had some pleasant companion who had agreed to tread life's path together with him; and this companion was none other than the overcoat with its thick cotton-wool padding and strong lining, made to last a lifetime. He livened up and, like a man who has set himself a goal, became more determined.

His indecision and uncertainty—in short, the vague and hesitant side of his personality—just disappeared of its own accord. At times a fire shone in his eyes, and even such daring and audacious thoughts as: 'Now, what about having a *marten* collar?' flashed through his mind.

All these reflections very nearly turned his mind. Once he was not far from actually making a *copying mistake*, so that he almost cried out 'Ugh!' and crossed himself. At least once a month he went to Petrovich's to see how the overcoat was getting on and to inquire where was the best place to buy cloth, what colour they should choose, and what price they should pay. Although slightly worried, he always returned home contented, thinking of the day when all the material would be bought and the overcoat finished. Things progressed quicker than he had ever hoped. The Director allowed Akaky Akakievich not forty or forty-five, but a whole *sixty* roubles bonus, which was beyond his wildest expectations. Whether that was because the Director had some premonition that he needed a new overcoat, or whether it was just pure chance, Akaky Akakievich found himself with an extra twenty roubles. And as a result every thing was speeded up. After another two or three months of mild starvation Akaky Akakievich had saved up the eighty roubles. His heart, which usually had a very steady beat, started pounding away. The very next day off he went shopping with Petrovich. They bought some *very* fine material, and no wonder, since they had done nothing but discuss it for the past six months and scarcely a month had gone by without their calling in at all the shops to compare prices. What was more, even Petrovich said you could not buy better cloth anywhere. For the lining they simply chose calico, but calico so strong and of such high quality that, according to Petrovich, it was finer than silk and even had a smarter and glossier look.

They did not buy marten for the collar, because it was really too expensive, but instead they settled on cat fur, the finest cat they could find in the shops and which could easily be mistaken for marten from a distance. In all, Petrovich took two weeks to finish the overcoat as there was so much quilting to be done. Otherwise it would have been ready much sooner. Petrovich charged twelve roubles—anything less was out of the question. He had used silk thread everywhere, with fine double seams, and had gone over them with his teeth afterwards to make different patterns.

It was ... precisely *which* day it is difficult to say, but without any doubt it was the most triumphant day in Akaky

Akakievich's whole life when Petrovich at last delivered the overcoat. He brought it early in the morning, even before Akaky Akakievich had left for the office. The overcoat could not have arrived at a better time, since fairly severe frosts had already set in and were likely to get even worse. Petrovich delivered the overcoat in person—just as a good tailor should. Akaky Akakievich had never seen him looking so solemn before. He seemed to know full well that his was no mean achievement, and that he had suddenly shown by his own work the gulf separating tailors who only relined or patched up overcoats from those who make new ones, right from the beginning. He took the overcoat out of the large kerchief he had wrapped it in and which he had only just got back from the laundry. Then he folded the kerchief and put it in his pocket ready for use. Then he took the overcoat very proudly in both hands and threw it very deftly round Akaky Akakievich's shoulders. He gave it a sharp tug, smoothed it downwards on the back, and draped it round Akaky Akakievich, leaving some buttons in the front undone. Akaky Akakievich, who was no longer a young man, wanted to try it with his arms in the sleeves. Petrovich helped him, and even this way it was the right size. In short, the overcoat was a perfect fit, without any shadow of doubt. Petrovich did not forget to mention it was only *because* he happened to live in a small backstreet and *because* his workship had no sign outside, and *because* he had known Akaky Akakievich such a long time, that he had charged him such a low price. If he had gone anywhere along Nevsky Avenue they would have rushed him seventy-five roubles for the labour alone. Akaky Akakievich did not feel like taking Petrovich up on this and in fact was rather intimidated by the large sums Petrovich was so fond of mentioning just to try and impress his clients. He settled up with him, thanked him and went straight off to the office in his new overcoat. Petrovich followed him out into the street, stood there for a long time having a look at the overcoat from some way off, and then deliberately made a small detour up a side street so that he could have a good view of the overcoat from the other side, i.e. coming straight towards him.

Meanwhile Akaky Akakievich continued on his way to the office in the most festive mood. Not one second passed without his being conscious of the new overcoat on his shoulders, and several times he even smiled from inward pleasure. And really the overcoat's advantages were two-fold: firstly, it was warm; secondly, it made him feel good. He did not notice where he was going at all and suddenly found himself at the office. In the lobby he took the overcoat off, carefully examined it all over, and then handed it to the porter for special safe-keeping.

No one knew how the news suddenly got round that Akaky Akakievich had a new overcoat and that his 'dressing-gown' was now no more. The moment he arrived everyone rushed out into the lobby to look at his new acquisition. They so overwhelmed him with congratulations and good wishes that he smiled at first and then he even began to feel quite embarrassed. When they all crowded round him saying they should have a drink on the new overcoat, and insisting that the *very least* he could do was to hold a party for all of them, Akaky Akakievich lost his head completely, not knowing what to do or what to answer or how to escape. Blushing all over, he tried for some considerable time, rather naïvely, to convince them it was not a new overcoat at all but really his old one. In the end one of the civil servants, who was nothing less than an assistant head clerk, and who was clearly anxious to show he was not at all snooty and could hobnob even with his inferiors, said: All right then, *I'll* throw a party instead. You're all invited over to my place this evening. It so happens it's my name-day.'

Naturally the others immediately offered the assistant head clerk their congratulations and eagerly accepted the invitation. When Akaky Akakievich tried to talk himself out of it, everyone said it was impolite, in fact quite shameful, and a refusal was out of the question. Later, however, he felt pleased when he remembered that the party would give him the opportunity of going out in his new overcoat that very same evening.

The whole day was like a triumphant holiday for Akaky Akakievich. He went home in the most jubilant mood, took off his coat, hung it up very carefully and stood there for some time admiring the cloth and lining. Then, to compare the two, he brought out his old 'dressing-gown', which by now had completely disintegrated. As he examined it he could not help laughing: what a *fantastic* difference! All through dinner the thought of his old overcoat and its shocking state made him smile. He ate his meal with great relish and afterwards did not do any copying but indulged in the luxury of lying on his bed until it grew dark. Then, without any further delay, he put his clothes on, threw his overcoat over his shoulders and went out into the street. Unfortunately the author cannot say exactly where the civil servant who was giving the party lived: his memory is beginning to let him down badly and everything in Petersburg, every house, every street, has become so blurred and mixed up in his mind that he finds it extremely difficult to say where *anything* is at all. All the same, we do at least know for certain that the civil servant lived in the *best part* of the city, which amounts to saying that he lived miles and miles away from Akaky Akakievich. At first Akaky Akakievich had to pass through some badly lit, deserted streets, but the nearer he got to the civil servant's flat the more lively and crowded they became, and the brighter the lamps shone. More and more people dashed by and he began to meet beautifully dressed ladies, and men with beaver collars. Here there were not so many cheap cabmen with their wooden basketwork sleighs studded with gilt nails. Instead, there were dashing coachmen with elegant cabs, wearing crimson velvet caps, their sleighs lacquered and covered with bearskins. Carriages with draped boxes simply flew down the streets with their wheels screeching over the snow.

Akaky Akakievich surveyed this scene as though he had never witnessed anything like it in his life. For some years now he had not ventured out at all in the evenings.

Filled with curiosity, he stopped by a brightly lit shop window to look at a painting of a pretty girl who was taking off her shoe and showing her entire leg, which was not at all bad-looking, while behind her a gentleman with side-whiskers and a fine goatee was poking his head round the door of an adjoining room. Akaky Akakievich shook his head and smiled, then went on his way. Why did he smile? Perhaps because this was something he had never set eyes on before, but for which, nonetheless, each one of us has some instinctive feeling. Or perhaps, like many other civil servants he thought: 'Oh, those Frenchmen! Of course, if they happen to fancy something, then really, I mean to say, to be exact, something . . .' Perhaps he was not thinking this at all, for it is impossible to probe deep into a man's soul and discover all his thoughts. Finally he arrived at the assistant head clerk's flat. This assistant head clerk lived in the grand style: a lamp shone on the staircase, and the flat was on the first floor.

As he entered the hall Akaky Akakievich saw row upon row of galoshes. Among them, in the middle of the room, stood a samovar, hissing as it sent out clouds of steam. The walls were covered with overcoats and cloaks; some of them even had beaver collars or velvet lapels. From the other side of the wall he could hear the buzzing of voices, which suddenly became loud and clear when the door opened and there emerged a footman carrying a tray laden with empty glasses, a jug of cream and a basketful of biscuits. There was no doubt at all that the clerks had been there a long time and had already drunk their first cup of tea.

When Akaky Akakievich had hung up his overcoat himself he went in and was struck all at once by the sight of candles, civil servants, pipes and card tables. His ears were filled with the blurred sound of little snatches of conversation coming from all over the room and the noise of chairs being shifted backwards and forwards. He stood very awkwardly in the middle of the room, looking around and trying to think what to do. But they had already spotted him and greeted him with loud shouts, everyone immediately crowding into the hall to have another look at the overcoat. Although he was somewhat overwhelmed by this reception, since he was a rather simpleminded and ingenuous person, he could not help feeling glad at the praises showered on his overcoat. And then, it goes without saying, they abandoned him, overcoat included, and turned their attention to the customary whist tables. All the noise and conversation and crowds of people—this was a completely new world for Akaky Akakievich. He simply did not know what to do, where to put his hands or feet or any other part of himself. Finally he took a seat near the cardplayers, looking at the cards, and examining first one player's face, then another's. In no time at all he started yawning and began to feel bored, especially as it was long after his usual bedtime.

He tried to take leave of his host, but everyone insisted on his staying to toast the new overcoat with a glassful of champagne. About an hour later supper was served. This consisted of mixed salad, cold veal, meat pasties, pastries and champagne. They made Akaky Akakievich drink two glasses, after which everything seemed a lot merrier, although he still could not forget that it was already midnight and that he should have left ages ago.

So that his host should not stop him on the way out, he crept silently from the room, found his overcoat in the hall (much to his regret it was lying on the floor), shook it to remove every trace of fluff, put it over his shoulders and went down the stairs into the street.

Outside it was still lit-up. A few small shops, which houseserfs and different kinds of people use as clubs at all hours of the day were open. Those which were closed had broad beams of light coming from chinks right the way down their doors, showing that there were still people talking inside, most probably maids and menservants who had not finished exchanging the latest gossip, leaving their masters completely in the dark as to where they had got to. Akaky Akakievich walked along in high spirits, and once, heavens know why, very nearly gave chase to some lady who flashed by like lightning, every part of her body showing an extraordinary mobility. However, he stopped in his tracks and continued at his previous leisurely pace, amazed at himself for breaking into that inexplicable trot. Soon there stretched before him those same empty streets which looked forbidding enough even in the daytime, let alone at night. Now they looked even more lonely and deserted. The street lamps thinned out more and more—the local council was stingy with its oil in this part of the town. Next he began to pass by wooden houses and fences. Not a soul anywhere, nothing but the snow gleaming in the streets and the cheerless dark shapes of low-built huts which, with their shutters closed, seemed to be asleep. He was now quite near the spot where the street was interrupted by an endless square with the houses barely visible on the other side: a terrifying desert. In the distance, God knows where, a light glimmered in a watchman's hut which seemed to be standing on the very edge of the world. At this point Akaky Akakievich's high spirits drooped considerably. As he walked out on to the square, he could not suppress the feeling of dread that welled up inside him, as though he sensed that something evil was going to happen. He looked back, then to both sides: it was as though he was surrounded by a whole ocean. 'No, it's best not to look,' he thought, and continued on his way with his eyes shut. When at last he opened them to see how much further he had to go he suddenly saw two men with moustaches right in front of him, although it was too dark to make them out exactly. His eyes misted over and his heart started pounding.

'Aha, that's *my* overcoat all right,' one of them said in a thunderous voice, grabbing him by the collar. Akaky Akakievich was about to shout for help, but the other man stuck a fist the size of a clerk's head right in his face and said: 'Just one squeak out of you!' All Akaky Akakievich knew was that they pulled his coat off and shoved a knee into him, making him fall backwards in the snow, after which he knew nothing more. A few minutes later he came to and managed to stand up, but by then there was no one to be seen. All he knew was that he was freezing and that his overcoat had gone, and he started shouting. But his voice would not carry across the vast square. Not once did he stop shouting as he ran desperately across the square towards a sentry box where a policeman stood propped up on his halberd looking rather intrigued as to who the devil was shouting and running towards him. When he had reached the policeman Akaky Akakievich (in between breathless gasps) shouted accusingly that he had been asleep, that he was neglecting his duty and could not even see when a man was being robbed under his very nose. The policeman replied that he had seen nothing, except for two men who had stopped him in the middle of the square and whom he had taken for his friends; and that instead of letting off steam he would be better advised to go the very next day to see the Police Inspector, who would get his overcoat back for him. Akaky Akakievich ran off home in the most shocking state: his hair—there was still some growing around the temples and the back of his head—was terribly dishevelled. His chest, his trousers, and his sides were covered with snow. When his old landlady heard a terrifying knocking at the door she leaped out of bed and rushed downstairs with only one shoe on, clutching her nightdress to her bosom out of modesty. But when she opened the door and saw the state Akaky Akakievich was in, she shrank backwards. After he had told her what had happened she clasped her hands in despair and told him to go straight to the District Police Superintendent, as the local officer was sure to try and put one over on him, make all kinds of promises and lead him right up the garden path. The best thing was to go direct to the Superintendent himself, whom she actually happened to know, as Anna, the Finnish girl who used to cook for her, was now a nanny at the Superintendent's house. She often saw him go past the houses and every Sunday he went to church, smiled at everyone as he prayed and to all intents and purposes was a thoroughly nice man. Akaky Akakievich listened to this advice and crept sadly up to his room. What sort of night he spent can best be judged by those who are able to put themselves in someone else's place. Early next morning he went to the Superintendent's house but was told that he was asleep. He returned at ten o'clock, but was informed that he was still asleep. He came back at eleven, and was told that he had gone out. When he turned up once again round about lunchtime, the clerks in the entrance hall would not let him through on any account, unless he told them first what his business was, why he had come, and what had happened. So in the end Akaky Akakievich, for the first time in his life, stood up for himself and told them in no uncertain terms that he wanted to see the Superintendent *in person*, that they dare not turn him away since he had come from a government department, and that they would know all about it if he made a complaint. The clerks did not have the nerve to argue and one of them went to fetch the Superintendent who reacted extremely strangely to the robbery. Instead of sticking to the main point of the story, he started cross-examining Akaky Akakievich with such questions as: 'What was he doing out so late?' or 'Had he been visiting a brothel?', which left Akaky feeling very embarrassed, and he went away completely in the dark as to whether they were going to take any action or not. The whole of that day he stayed away from the office—for the first time in his life.

The next morning he arrived looking very pale and wearing his old dressing-gown, which was in an even more pathetic state.

The story of the stolen overcoat touched many of the clerks, although a few of them could not refrain from laughing at Akaky Akakievich even then. There and then they decided to make a collection, but all they raised was a miserable little sum since, apart from any *extra* expense, they had nearly exhausted all their funds subscribing to a new portrait of the Director as well as to some book or other recommended by one of the heads of department—who happened to be a friend of the author. So they collected next to nothing.

One of them, who was deeply moved, decided he could at least help Akaky Akakievich with some good advice. He told him not to go to the local police officer, since although that gentleman might well recover his overcoat somehow or other in the hope of receiving a recommendation from his superiors, Akaky did not have a chance of getting it out of the police station without the necessary legal proof that the overcoat was really his. The best plan was to apply to a certain *Important Person*, and this same Important Person, by writing to and contacting the proper people, would get things moving much faster. There was nothing else for it, so Akaky Akakievich decided to go and see this Important Person.

What exactly this Important Person did and what position he held remains a mystery to this day. All we need say is that this Important Person had become important only a short while before, and that until then he had been an *unimportant* person. However, even now his position was not considered very important if compared with others which were still more important. But you will always come across a certain class of people who consider something unimportant which for other people is in fact important. However, he tried all manners and means of buttressing his importance. For example, he was responsible for introducing the rule that all low-ranking civil servants should be waiting to meet him on the stairs when he arrived at the office; that no one, on any account, could walk straight into his office; and that everything must be dealt with in the *strictest* order of priority: the collegiate registrar was to report to the provincial secretary who in turn was to report to the titular councillor (or whoever it was he *had* to report to) so that in this way the matter reached him according to the prescribed procedure. In this Holy Russia of ours everything is infected by a mania for imitation, and everyone apes his superior. I have even heard say that when a certain titular councillor was appointed head of some minor government department he immediately partitioned off a section of his office into a special room for himself, an 'audience chamber' as he called it, and made two ushers in uniforms with red collars and gold braid stand outside to open the doors for visitors—even though you would have a job getting an ordinary writing desk into this so-called chamber.

This Important Person's routine was very imposing and impressive, but nonetheless simple. The whole basis of his system was strict discipline. 'Discipline, discipline, and ... discipline' he used to say, usually looking very solemnly into the face of the person he was addressing when he had repeated this word for the third time. However, there was really no good reason for this strict discipline, since the ten civil servants or so who made up the whole administrative machinery of his department were all duly terrified of him anyway. If they saw him coming from some way off they would stop what they were doing and stand to attention while the Director went through the office. His normal everyday conversation with his subordinates simply *reeked* of discipline and consisted almost entirely of three phrases: 'How dare you? Do you know who you're talking to? Do you realize who's standing before you?'

However, he was quite a good man at heart, pleasant to his colleagues and helpful. But his promotion to general's rank had completely turned his head; he became all mixed up, somehow went off the rails, and just could not cope any more. If he happened to be with someone of equal rank, then he was quite a normal person, very decent in fact and indeed far from stupid in many respects.

But put him with people only one rank lower, and he was really at sea. He would not say a single word, and one felt sorry to see him in such a predicament, all the more so as even *he* felt that he could have been spending the time far more enjoyably.

One could read this craving for interesting company and conversation in his eyes, but he was always inhibited by the thought: would this be going too far for someone in his position, would this be showing too much familiarity and therefore rather damaging to his status? For these reasons he would remain perpetually silent, producing a few monosyllables from time to time, and as a result acquired the reputation of being a terrible bore. This was the Important Person our Akaky Akakievich went to consult, and he appeared at the worst possible moment—most inopportune as far as *he* was concerned—but most opportune for the Important Person. The Important Person was in his office having a very animated talk with an old childhood friend who had just arrived in Petersburg and whom he had not seen for a few years.

At this moment the arrival of a certain Bashmachkin was announced. 'Who's he?' he asked abruptly and was told, 'Some clerk or other.' 'Ah, let him wait, I can't see him just now,' the Important Person replied. Here we should say that the Important Person told a complete lie: he had plenty of time, he had long since said all he wanted to his friend, and for some considerable time their conversation had been punctuated by very long silences broken only by their slapping each other on the thigh and saying:

'Quite so, Ivan Abramovich!' and 'Well yes, Stepan Varlamovich!'

Even so, he still ordered the clerk to wait, just to show his old friend (who had left the Service a fair time before and was now nicely settled in his country house) how long he could keep clerks standing about in his waiting-room. When they really had said all that was to be said, or rather, had sat there in the very comfortable easy chairs to their heart's content without saying a single word to each other, puffing away at their cigars, the Important Person suddenly remembered and told his secretary, who was standing by the door with a pile of papers in his hands: 'Ah yes now, I think there's some clerk or other waiting out there. Tell him to come in.' One look at the timid Akaky Akakievich in his ancient uniform and he suddenly turned towards him and said: 'What do *you* want?' in that brusque and commanding voice he had been practising especially, when he was alone in his room, in front of a mirror, a whole week before his present appointment and promotion to general's rank.

Long before this Akaky Akakievich had been experiencing that feeling of awe which it was proper and necessary for him to experience, and now, somewhat taken aback, he tried to explain, as far as his tongue wold allow him and with an even greater admixture than ever before of 'wells' and 'that is to says', that his overcoat was a new one, that he had been robbed in the most barbarous manner, that he had come to ask the Important Person's help, so that through his influence, or by doing this or that, by writing to the Chief of Police or someone else (whoever it might be), the Important Person might get his overcoat back for him.

Heaven knows why, but the general found this approach rather too familiar.

'What do you mean by this, sir?' he snapped again. 'Are you unaware of the correct procedure? Where do you think you are? Don't you know how things are conducted here? It's high time you knew that first of all your application must be handed in at the main office, then taken to the chief clerk, then to the departmental director, then to my secretary, who *then* submits it to me for consideration . . .'

'But Your Excellency,' said Akaky Akakievich, trying to

summon up the small handful of courage he possessed, and feeling at the same time that the sweat was pouring off him, 'I took the liberty of disturbing Your Excellency because, well, secretaries, you know, are a rather unreliable lot . . .'

'What, what, what?' cried the Important Person. 'Where did you learn such impudence? Where did you get those ideas from? What rebellious attitude has infected the young men these days?'

Evidently the Important Person did not notice that Akaky Akakievich was well past fifty. Of course, one might call him a young man, relatively speaking; that is, if you compared him with someone of seventy.

'Do you realize who you're talking to? Do you know who is standing before you? Do you understand, I ask you, do you understand? I'm asking you a question!'

At this point he stamped his foot and raised his voice to such a pitch that Akaky Akakievich was not the only one to be scared out of his wits. Akaky Akakievich almost fainted. He reeled forward, his body shook all over and he could hardly stand on his feet. If the porters had not rushed to his assistance he would have fallen flat on the floor. He was carried out almost lifeless. The Important Person, very satisfied that the effect he had produced exceeded even *his* wildest expectations, and absolutely delighted that a few words from him could deprive a man of his senses, peeped at his friend out of the corner of one eye to see what impression he had made. He was not exactly displeased to see that his friend was quite bewildered and was even beginning to show unmistakable signs of fear himself.

Akaky Akakievich remembered nothing about going down the stairs and out into the street. His hands and feet had gone dead. Never in his life had he received such a savage dressing-down from a general—and what is more, a general from another department.

He continually stumbled off the pavement as he struggled on with his mouth wide open in the face of a raging blizzard that whistled down the street. As it normally does in St Petersburg the wind was blowing from all four corners of the earth and from every single side-street. In a twinkling his throat was inflamed and when he finally dragged himself home he was unable to say one word. He put himself to bed and broke out all over in swellings. That is what a 'proper and necessary' dressing-down can sometimes do for you!

The next day he had a high fever. Thanks to the generous assistance of the Petersburg climate the illness made much speedier progress than one might have expected, and when the doctor arrived and felt his pulse, all he could prescribe was a poultice—and only then for the simple reason that he did not wish his patient to be deprived of the salutary benefits of medical aid. However, he *did* advance the diagnosis that Akaky Akakievich would not last another day and a half, no doubt about that, and then: *kaput*. After which he turned to the landlady and said:

'Now, don't waste any time and order a pine coffin right away, as he won't be able to afford oak.'

Whether Akaky Akakievich heard these fateful words—and if he did hear them, whether they shocked him into some feeling of regret for his wretched life—no one has the slightest idea, since he was feverish and delirious the whole time. Strange visions, each weirder than the last, paraded endlessly before him: in one he could see Petrovich the tailor and he was begging him to make an overcoat with special traps to catch thieves that seemed to be swarming under his bed. Every other minute he called out to his landlady to drag one out which had actually crawled under the blankets.

In another he was asking why his old 'dressing-gown' was hanging up there when he had a *new* overcoat. Then he imagined himself standing next to the general and, after being duly and properly reprimanded, saying: 'I'm sorry, Your Excellency.' In the end he started cursing and swearing and let forth such a torrent of terrible obscenities that his good landlady crossed herself, as she had never heard the like from him in all her born days, especially as the curses always seemed to follow right after those 'Your Excellencies'. Later on he began to talk complete gibberish, until it was impossible to understand anything, except that this jumble of words and thoughts always centered on one and the same overcoat. Finally poor Akaky Akakievich gave up the ghost. Neither his room nor what he had in the way of belonging was sealed off, in the first place, because he had no family, and in the second place, because his worldly possessions did not amount to very much at all: a bundle of goose quills, one quire of white government paper, three pairs of socks, two or three buttons that had come off his trousers, and the 'dressing-gown' with which the reader is already familiar. Whom all this went to, God only knows, and the author of this story confesses that he is not even interested. Akaky Akakievich was carted away and buried. And St Petersburg carried on without its Akaky Akakievich just as though he had never even existed.

So vanished and disappeared for ever a human being whom no one ever thought of protecting, who was dear to no one, in whom no one was the least interested, not even the naturalist who cannot resist sticking a pin in a common fly and examining it under the microscope; a being who endured the mockery of his colleagues without protesting, who went to his grave without any undue fuss, but to whom, nonetheless (although not until his last days) a shining visitor in the form of an overcoat suddenly appeared, brightening his wretched life for one fleeting moment; a being upon whose head disaster had cruelly fallen, just as it falls upon the kings and great ones of this earth . . .

A few days after his death a messenger was sent with instructions for him to report to the office *immediately:* it was the Director's own orders. But the messenger was obliged to return on his own and announced that Akaky would not be coming any more. When asked when not he replied: ' 'Cos 'e's dead, bin dead these four days.' This was how the office got to know about Akaky Akakievich's death, and on the very next day his place was taken by a new clerk, a much taller man whose handwriting was not nearly so upright and indeed had a pronounced slope.

But who would have imagined that this was not the last of Akaky Akakievich, and that he was destined to create quite a stir several days after his death, as though he were trying to make up for a life spent being ignored by everybody? But this is what happened and it provides our miserable story with a totally unexpected, fantastic ending. Rumours suddenly started going round St Petersburg that a ghost in the form of a government clerk had been seen near the Kalinkin Bridge, and even further afield, and that this ghost appeared to be searching for a lost overcoat. To this end it was to be seen ripping all kinds of overcoats from everyone's shoulders, with no regard for rank or title: overcoats made from cat fur, beaver, quilted overcoats, raccoon, fox, bear—in short, overcoats made from every conceivable fur or skin that man has ever used to protect his own hide. One of the clerks from the department saw the ghost with his own eyes and immediately recognized it as Akaky Akakievich. He was so terrified that he ran off as fast as his legs would carry him, with the result he did not manage to have a very good look: all he could make out was someone pointing a menacing finger at him from the distance. Complaints continually poured in from all quarters, not only from titular councillors, but even from such high-ranking officials as privy councillors, who were being subjected to quite nasty colds in the back through this nocturnal ripping off of their overcoats. The police were instructed to run the ghost in, come what may, dead or alive, and to punish it most severely, as an example to others—and in this they very nearly succeeded. To be precise, a policeman, part of whose beat lay along Kirushkin Alley, was on the point of grabbing the ghost by the collar at the very scene of the crime, just as he was about to tear a woollen overcoat from the shoulder of a retired musician who, in his day, used to tootle on the flute. As he seized the ghost by the collar the policeman shouted to two of his friends to come and keep hold of it, just for a minute, while he felt in his boot for his birch-bark snuff-box to revive his nose (which had been slightly frost-bitten six times in his life). But the snuff must have been one of those blends even a ghost could not stand, for the policeman had barely managed to cover his right nostril with a finger and sniff half a handful up the other when the ghost sneezed so violently that they were completely blinded by the spray, all three of them. While they were wiping their eyes the ghost disappeared into thin air, so suddenly that the policemen could not even say for certain if they had ever laid hands on it in the first place. From then on the local police were so scared of ghosts that they were frightened of arresting even the living and would shout instead: 'Hey you, clear off!'—from a safe distance.

The clerk's ghost began to appear even far beyond the Kalinkin Bridge, causing no little alarm and apprehension among fainter-hearted citizens. However, we seem to have completely neglected the Important Person, who, in fact, could almost be said to be the *real* reason for the fantastic turn this otherwise authentic story has taken. First of all, to give him his due, we should mention that soon after the departure of our poor shattered Akaky Akakievich the Important Person felt some twinges of regret. Compassion was not something new to him, and, although consciousness of his rank very often stifled them, his heart was not untouched by many generous impulses. As soon as his friend had left the office his thoughts turned to poor Akaky Akakievich.

Almost every day after that he had visions of the pale Akaky Akakievich, for whom an official wigging had been altogether too much. These thoughts began to worry him to such an extent that a week later he decided to send someone round from the office to the flat to ask how he was and if he could be of any help. When the messenger reported that Akaky Akakievich had died suddenly of a fever he was quite stunned. His conscience began troubling him, and all that day he felt off-colour.

Thinking that some light entertainment might help him forget that unpleasant experience he went off to a party given by one of his friends which was attended by quite a respectable crowd. He was particularly pleased to see that everyone there held roughly the same rank as himself, so there was no chance of any embarrassing situations. All this had an amazingly uplifting effect on his state of mind. He unwound completely, chatted very pleasantly, made himself agreeable to everyone, and in short, spent a very pleasant evening. Over dinner he drank one or two glasses of champagne, a wine which, as everyone knows, is not exactly calculated to dampen high spirits. The champagne put him in the mood for introducing several changes in his plans for that evening: he decided not to go straight home, but to call on a lady of his acquaintance, Karolina Ivanovna, who was of German origin and with whom he was on the friendliest terms. Here I should mention that the Important Person was no longer a young man but a good husband and the respected head of a family. His two sons, one of whom already had a job in the Civil Service, and a sweet sixteen-year-old daughter with a pretty little turned-up nose, came every day to kiss his hand and say *'Bonjour, Papa'*. His wife, who still retained some of her freshness and had not even lost any of her good looks, allowed him to kiss her hand first, and then kissed his, turning it the other side up. But although the Important Person was thoroughly contented with the affection lavished on him by his family, he still did not think it wrong to have a lady friend in another part of the town. This lady friend was not in the least prettier or younger than his wife, but that is one of the mysteries of this world, and it is not for us to criticize. As I was saying, the Important Person went downstairs, climbed into his sledge and said to the driver: 'To Karolina

Ivanovna's', while he wrapped himself snugly in his warm, very luxurious overcoat, revelling in that happy state of mind, so very dear to Russians, when one is thinking about absolutely nothing, but when, nonetheless, thoughts come crowding into one's head of their own accord, each more delightful than the last, and not even requiring one to make the mental effort of conjuring them up or chasing after them. He felt very contented as he recalled, without any undue exertion, all the gayest moments of the party, all the *bons mots* that had aroused loud guffaws in that little circle: some of them he even repeated quietly to himself and found just as funny as before, so that it was not at all surprising that he laughed very heartily. The boisterous wind, however, interfered with his enjoyment at times: blowing up God knows where or why, it cut right into his face, hurling lumps of snow at it, making his collar billow out like a sail, or blowing it back over his head with such supernatural force that he had the devil's own job extricating himself. Suddenly the Important Person felt a violent tug at his collar. Turning round, he saw a smallish man in an old, worn-out uniform, and not without a feeling of horror recognized him as Akaky Akakievich. The clerk's face was as pale as the snow and was just like a dead man's.

The Important Person's terror passed all bounds when the ghost's mouth became twisted, smelling horribly of the grave as it breathed on him and pronounced the following words: 'Ah, at last I've found you! Now I've, er, him, collared you!

It's *your* overcoat I'm after! You didn't care about mine, *and* you couldn't resist giving me a good ticking-off into the bargain! Now hand over *your* overcoat!' The poor Important Person nearly died. However much strength of character he displayed in the office (usually in the presence of his subordinates)—one only had to look at his virile face and bearing to say: '*There*'s a man for you!'—in this situation, like many of his kind who seem heroic at first sight, he was so frightened that he even began to fear (and not without reason) that he was in for a heart attack. He tore off his overcoat as fast as he could, without any help, and then shouted to his driver in a terrified voice: 'Home as fast as you can!'

The driver, recognizing the tone of voice his master used only in moments of crisis—a tone of voice usually accompanied by some much stronger encouragement—just to be on the safe side hunched himself up, flourished his whip and shot off like an arrow.

Not much more than six minutes later the Important Person was already at his front door. He was coatless, terribly pale and frightened out of his wits, and had driven straight home instead of going to Karolina Ivanovna's. Somehow he managed to struggle up to his room and spent a very troubled night, so much so that next morning his daughter said to him over breakfast: 'You look very pale today, Papa.' But Papa did not reply, did not say a single word to anyone about what had happened, where he had been and where he had originally intended going. The encounter had made a deep impression on him. From that time onwards he would seldom say: 'How dare you! Do you realize who is standing before you?' to his subordinates. And if he did have occasion to say this, it was never without first hearing what the accused had to say. But what was more surprising than anything else the ghostly clerk disappeared completely. Obviously the general's overcoat was a perfect fit. At least, there were no more stories about overcoats being torn off people's backs. However, many officious and over-cautious citizens would not be satisfied, insisting the ghost could still be seen in the remoter parts of the city, and in fact a certain police constable from the Kolomna district saw with his own eyes a ghost leaving a house. However, being rather weakly built—once a quite normal-sized, fully mature piglet which came tearing out of a private house knocked him off his feet, to the huge amusement of some cab-drivers who were standing near by, each of whom was made to cough up half a kopeck in snuff-money for his cheek—he simply did not have the nerve to make an arrest, but followed the ghost in the dark until it suddenly stopped, turned round, asked: 'What do *you* want?' and shook its fist at him—a fist the like of which you will never see in the land of the living. The constable replied: 'Nothing', and beat a hasty retreat. This ghost, however, was much taller than the first, had an absolutely enormous moustache and, apparently heading towards the Obukhov Bridge, was swallowed up in the darkness.

The Nose

An extraordinarily strange thing happened in St Petersburg on 25 March. Ivan Yakovlevich, a barber who lived on Voznesensky Avenue (his surname has got lost and all that his shop-front signboard shows is a gentleman with a lathered cheek and the inscription 'We also let blood'), woke up rather early one morning and smelt hot bread. As he sat up in bed he saw his wife, who was a quite respectable lady and a great coffee-drinker, taking some freshly baked rolls out of the oven.

'I don't want any coffee today, Praskovya Osipovna,' said Ivan Yakovlevich, 'I'll make do with some hot rolls and onion instead.' (Here I must explain that Ivan Yakovlevich would really have liked to have had some coffee as well, but knew it was quite out of the question to expect both coffee *and* rolls, since Praskovya Osipovna did not take very kindly to these whims of his.) 'Let the old fool have his bread, I don't mind,' she thought. 'That means extra coffee for me!' And she threw a roll on to the table.

Ivan pulled his frock-coat over his nightshirt for decency's sake, sat down at the table, poured out some salt, peeled two onions, took a knife and with a determined expression on his face started cutting one of the rolls.

When he had sliced the roll in two, he peered into the middle and was amazed to see something white there. Ivan carefully picked at it with his knife, and felt it with his finger. 'Quite thick,' he said to himself. 'What on earth can it be?'

He poked two fingers in and pulled out—a nose!

He flopped back in his chair, and began rubbing his eyes and feeling around in the roll again. Yes, it was a nose all right, no mistake about that. And, what's more, it seemed a very familiar nose. His face filled with horror. But this horror was nothing compared with his wife's indignation.

'You beast, whose nose is *that* you've cut off?' she cried furiously. 'You scoundrel! You drunkard! I'll report it to the police myself, I will. You thief! Come to think of it, I've heard three customers say that when they come in for a shave you start pulling their noses about so much it's a wonder they stay on at all!'

But Ivan felt more dead than alive. He knew that the nose belonged to none other than Collegiate Assessor Kovalyov, whom he shaved on Wednesdays and Sundays.

'Wait a minute, Praskovya! I'll wrap it up in a piece of cloth and dump it in the corner. Let's leave it there for a bit, then I'll try and get rid of it.'

'I don't want to know! Do you think I'm going to let a sawn-off nose lie around in *my* room . . . you fathead! All you can do is stop that blasted razor of yours and let everything else go to pot. Layabout! Night-bird! And you expect me to cover up for you with the police! You filthy pig! Blockhead! Get that nose out of here, out! Do what you like with it, but I don't want that thing hanging around here a minute longer!'

Ivan Yakovlevich was absolutely stunned. He thought and thought, but just didn't know what to make of it.

'I'm damned if I know what's happened!' he said at last, scratching the back of his ear. 'I can't say for certain if I came home drunk or not last night. All I know is, it's crazy. After all, bread is baked in an oven, and you don't get noses in bakeries. Can't make head or tail of it! . . .'

Ivan Yakovlevich lapsed into silence. The thought that the police might search the place, find the nose and afterwards bring a charge against him, very nearly sent him out of his mind. Already he could see that scarlet collar beautifully embroidered with silver, that sword . . . and he began shaking all over. Finally he put on his scruffy old trousers and shoes and with Praskovya Osipovna's vigorous invective ringing in his ears, wrapped the nose up in a piece of cloth and went out into the street.

All he wanted was to stuff it away somewhere, either hiding it between two curb-stones by someone's front door or else 'accidentally' dropping it and slinking off down a side street. But as luck would have it, he kept bumping into friends, who would insist on asking: 'Where are *you* off to?'

or 'It's a bit early for shaving customers, isn't it?' with the result that he didn't have a chance to get rid of it. Once he *did* manage to drop it, but a policeman pointed with his halberd and said: 'Pick that up! Can't you see you dropped something!' And Ivan Yakovlevich had to pick it up and hide it in his pocket. Despair gripped him, especially as the streets were getting more and more crowded now as the shops and stalls began to open.

He decided to make his way to St Isaac's Bridge and see if he could throw the nose into the River Neva without anyone seeing him. But here I am rather at fault for not telling you before something about Ivan Yakovlevich, who in many ways was a man you could respect.

Ivan Yakovlevich, like any honest Russian working man, was a terrible drunkard. And although he spent all day shaving other people's beards, he never touched his own. His frock-coat (Ivan Yakovlevich never wore a dress-coat) could best be described as piebald: that is to say, it was black, but with brownish-yellow and grey spots all over it. His collar was very shiny, and three loosely hanging threads showed that some buttons had once been there. Ivan Yakovlevich was a very phlegmatic character, and whenever Kovalyov the Collegiate Assessor said 'Your hands always stink!' while he was being shaved, Ivan Yakovlevich would say: 'But why *should* they stink?' The Collegiate Assessor used to reply: 'Don't ask me, my dear chap. All I know is, they *stink*.' Ivan Yakovlevich would answer by taking a pinch of snuff and then, by way of retaliation, lather all over Kovalyov's cheeks, under his nose, behind the ears and beneath his beard—in short, wherever he felt like covering him with soap.

By now this respectable citizen of ours had already reached St Isaac's Bridge. First of all he had a good look round. Then he leant over the rails, trying to pretend he was looking under the bridge to see if there were many fish there, and furtively threw the packet into the water. He felt as if a couple of hundredweight had been lifted from his shoulders and he even managed to produce a smile.

Instead of going off to shave civil servants' chins, he headed for a shop bearing the sign 'Hot Meals and Tea' for a glass of punch. Suddenly he saw a policeman at one end of the bridge, in a very smart uniform, with broad whiskers, a three-cornered hat and a sword. He went cold all over as the policeman beckoned to him and said: 'Come here, my friend!'

Recognizing the uniform, Ivan Yakovlevich took his cap off before he had taken half a dozen steps, tripped up to him and greeted him with: 'Good morning, Your Excellency!'

'No, no, my dear chap, none of your "Excellencies". Just tell me what you were up to on the bridge?'

'Honest, officer, I was on my way to shave a customer and stopped to see how fast the current was.'

'You're lying. You really can't expect me to believe that! You'd better come clean at once!'

'I'll give Your Excellency a free shave twice, even three times a week, honest I will,' answered Ivan Yakovlevich.

'No, no, my friend, that won't do. Three barbers look after me already, and it's an *honour* for them to shave me. Will you please tell me what you were up to?'

Ivan Yakovlevich turned pale . . . But at this point everything became so completely enveloped in mist it is really impossible to say what happened afterwards.

2

Collegiate Assessor Kovalyov woke up rather early and made a 'brring' noise with his lips. He always did this when he woke up, though, if you asked him why, he could not give any good reason. Kovalyov stretched himself and asked for the small mirror that stood on the table to be brought over to him. He wanted to have a look at a pimple that had made its appearance on his nose the previous evening, but to his extreme astonishment found that instead of a nose there was nothing but an absolutely flat surface! In a terrible panic Kovalyov asked for some water and rubbed his eyes with a towel. No mistake about it: his nose had gone. He began pinching himself to make sure he was not sleeping, but to all intents and purposes he was wide awake. Collegiate Assessor Kovalyov sprang out of bed and shook himself: still no nose! He asked for his clothes and off he dashed straight to the Head of Police.

In the meantime, however, a few words should be said about Kovalyov, so that the reader may see what kind of collegiate assessor this man was. You really cannot compare those collegiate assessors who acquire office through testimonials with the variety appointed in the Caucasus. The two species are quite distinct. Collegiate assessors with diplomas from learned bodies . . . But Russia is such an amazing country, that if you pass any remark about *one* collegiate assessor, every assessor from Riga to Kamchatka will take it personally. And the same goes for all people holding titles and government ranks. Kovalyov belonged to the Caucasian variety.

He had been a collegiate assessor for only two years and therefore could not forget it for a single minute. To make himself sound more important and to give more weight to his status he never called himself collegiate assessor, but 'Major'. If he met a woman in the street selling shirt fronts he would say: 'Listen dear, come and see me at home. My flat's in Sadovaya Street. All you have to do is ask if Major Kovalyov lives there and anyone will show you the way.' And if the woman was at all pretty he would whisper some secret instructions and then say: 'Just ask for Major Kovalyov, my dear.' Therefore, throughout this story, we will call this collegiate assessor 'Major.' Major Kovalyov was in the habit of taking a daily stroll along the Nevsky Avenue. His shirt collar was always immaculately clean and well-starched. His whiskers were the kind you usually find among provincial surveyors, architects and regimental surgeons, among people who have some sort of connection with the police, on anyone in fact who has full rosy cheeks and plays a good hand at whist. These whiskers grew right from the middle of his cheeks up to his nostrils. Major Kovalyov always carried plenty of seals with him—seals bearing coats of arms or engraved with the words: 'Wednesday, Thursday, Monday,' and so on. Major Kovalyov had come to St Petersburg with the set purpose of finding a position in keeping with his rank. If he was lucky, he would get a vice-governorship, but failing that, a job as an administrative clerk in some important government department would have to do. Major Kovalyov was not averse to marriage, as long as his bride happened to be worth 200,000 roubles. And now the reader can judge for himself how this Major felt when, instead of a fairly presentable and reasonably sized nose, all he saw was an absolutely preposterous smooth flat space.

As if this were not bad enough, there was not a cab in sight, and he had to walk home, keeping himself huddled up in his cloak and with a handkerchief over his face to make people think he was bleeding. 'But perhaps I dreamt it! How could I be so stupid as to go and lose my nose?' With these thoughts he dropped into a coffee-house to take a look at himself in a mirror. Fortunately the shop was empty, except for some waiters sweeping up and tidying the chairs. A few of them, rather bleary-eyed, were carrying trays laden with hot pies. Yesterday's newspapers, covered in coffee stains, lay scattered on the tables and chairs. 'Well, thank God there's no one about,' he said. 'Now I can have a look.' He approached the mirror rather gingerly and peered into it. 'Damn it! What kind of trick is this?' he cried, spitting on the floor. 'If only there were *something* to take its place, but there's nothing!'

He bit his lips in annoyance, left the coffee-house and decided not to smile or look at anyone, which was not like him at all. Suddenly he stood rooted to the spot near the front door of some house and witnessed a most incredible sight. A carriage drew up at the entrance porch. The doors flew open and out jumped a uniformed, stooping gentleman who dashed up the steps. The feeling of horror and amazement that gripped Kovalyov when he recognized his own nose defies description! After this extraordinary sight everything went topsy-turvy. He could hardly keep to his feet, but decided at all costs to wait until the nose returned to the carriage, although he was shaking all over and felt quite feverish.

About two minutes later a nose really did come out. It was wearing a gold-braided uniform with a high stand-up collar and chamois trousers, and had a sword at its side. From the plumes on its hat one could tell that it held the exalted rank of state councillor. And it was abundantly clear that the nose was going to visit someone. It looked right, then left, shouted to the coachman 'Let's go!', climbed in and drove off.

Poor Kovalyov nearly went out of his mind. He did not know what to make of it. How, in fact, could a nose, which only yesterday was in the middle of his face, and which could not possibly walk around or drive in a carriage, suddenly turn up in a uniform! He ran after the carriage which fortunately did not travel very far and came to a halt outside Kazan Cathedral. Kovalyov rushed into the cathedral square, elbowed his way through a crowd of beggar women who always used to make him laugh because of the way they covered their faces, leaving only slits for the eyes, and made his way in. Only a few people were at prayer, all of them standing by the entrance. Kovalyov felt so distraught that the was in no condition for praying, and his eyes searched every nook and cranny for the nose in uniform. At length he spotted it standing by one of the walls to the side. The nose's face was completely hidden by the high collar and it was praying with an expression of profound piety.

'What's the best way of approaching it?' thought Kovalyov. 'Judging by its uniform, its hat, and its whole appearance, it must be a state councillor. But I'm damned if I know!'

He tried to attract its attention by coughing, but the nose did not interrupt its devotions for one second and continued bowing towards the altar.

'My dear sir,' Kovalyov said, summoning up his courage, 'my dear sir . . .'

'What do you want?' replied the nose, turning round.

'I don't know how best to put it, sir, but it strikes me as very peculiar . . . Don't you know where you belong? And where do I find you? In church, of all places! I'm sure you'll agree that . . .'

'Please forgive me, but would you mind telling me what you're talking about? . . . Explain yourself.'

'How can I make myself clear?' Kovalyov wondered. Nerving himself once more he said: 'Of course, I am, as it happens, a Major. You will agree that it's not done for someone in my position to walk around minus a nose. It's all right for some old woman selling peeled oranges on the Voskresensky Bridge to go around without one. But as I'm hoping to be promoted soon . . . Besides, as I'm acquainted with several highly-placed ladies: Madame Chekhtaryev, for example, a state councillor's wife . . . you can judge for yourself . . . I really don't know what to say, my dear sir . . . (He shrugged his shoulders as he said this.) Forgive me, but you must look upon this as a matter of honour and principle. You can see for yourself . . .'

'I can't see anything,' the nose replied. 'Please come to the point.'

'My dear sir,' continued Kovalyov in a smug voice, 'I really don't know what you mean by that. It's plain enough for anyone to see . . . Unless you want . . . Don't you realize you are *my own nose!*'

The nose looked at the Major and frowned a little.

'My dear fellow, you are mistaken. I am a person in my own right. Furthermore, I don't see that we can have anything in common. Judging from your uniform buttons, I should say you're from another government department.'

With these words the nose turned away and continued its prayers.

Kovalyov was so confused he did not know what to do or think. At that moment he heard the pleasant rustling of a woman's dress, and an elderly lady, bedecked with lace, came by, accompanied by a slim girl wearing a white dress, which showed her shapely figure to very good advantage, and a pale yellow hat as light as pastry. A tall footman, with enormous whiskers and what seemed to be a dozen collars, stationed himself behind them and opened his snuff-box. Kovalyov went closer, pulled the linen collar of his shirt front up high, straightened the seals hanging on his gold watch chain and, smiling all over his face, turned his attention to the slim girl, who bent over to pray like a spring flower and kept lifting her little white hand with its almost transparent fingers to her forehead.

The smile on Kovalyov's face grew even more expansive when he saw, beneath her hat, a little rounded chin of dazzling white, and cheeks flushed with the colour of the first rose of spring.

But suddenly he jumped backwards as though he had been burnt: he remembered that instead of a nose he had nothing, and tears streamed from his eyes. He turned round to tell the nose in uniform straight out that it was only masquerading as a state councillor, that it was an impostor and a scoundrel, and really nothing else than his own private property, *his* nose ... But the nose had already gone: it had managed to slip off unseen, probably to pay somebody a visit.

This reduced Kovalyov to absolute despair. He went out, and stood for a minute or so under the colonnade, carefully looking around him in the hope of spotting the nose. He remembered quite distinctly that it was wearing a plumed hat and a gold-embroidered uniform. But he had not noticed what its greatcoat was like, or the colour of its carriage, or its horses, or even if there was a liveried footman at the back. What's more, there were so many carriages careering to and fro, so fast, that it was practically impossible to recognize any of them, and even if he could, there was no way of making them stop.

It was a beautiful sunny day. Nevsky Avenue was packed. From the Police Headquarters right down to the Anichkov Bridge people flowed along the pavements in a cascade of colour. Not far off he could see that court councillor whom he referred to as Lieutenant-Colonel, especially if there happened to be other people around. And over there was Yaygin, a head clerk in the Senate, and a very close friend of his who always lost at whist when he played in a party of eight. Another Major, a collegiate assessor, of the Caucasian variety, waved to him to come over and have a chat.

'Blast and damn!' said Kovalyov, hailing a drozhky. 'Driver, take me straight to the Chief of Police.'

He climbed into the drozhky and shouted: 'Drive like the devil!'

'Is the Police Commissioner in?' he said as soon as he entered the hall.

'No, he's not, sir,' said the porter. 'He left only a few minutes ago.'

'This really *is* my day.'

'Yes,' added the porter, 'you've only just missed him. A minute ago you'd have caught him.'

Kovalyov, his handkerchief still pressed to his face, climbed into the drozhky again and cried out in a despairing voice: 'Let's go!'

'Where?' asked the driver.

'Straight on!'

'Straight on? But it's a dead-end here—you can only go right or left.'

This last question made Kovalyov stop and think. In his position the best thing to do was to go first to the City Security Office, not because it was directly connected with the police, but because things got done there much quicker than in any other government department. There was no sense in going direct to the head of the department where the nose claimed to work since anyone could see from the answers he had got before that the nose considered nothing holy and would have no difficulty in convincing its superiors by its brazen lying that it had never set eyes on Kovalyov before.

So just as Kovalyov was about to tell the driver to go

straight to the Security Office, it struck him that the scoundrel and impostor who had behaved so shamelessly could quite easily take advantage of the delay and slip out of the city, in which event all his efforts to find it would be futile and might even drag on for another month, God forbid. Finally inspiration came from above. He decided to go straight to the newspaper offices and publish an advertisement, giving such a detailed description of the nose that anyone who happened to meet it would at once turn it over to Kovalyov, or at least tell him where he could find it. Deciding this was the best course of action, he ordered the driver to go straight to the newspaper offices and throughout the whole journey never once stopped pummelling the driver in the back with his fist and shouting: 'Faster, damn you, faster!'

'But sir . . .' the driver retorted as he shook his head and flicked his reins at his horse, which had a coat as long as a spaniel's. Finally the drozhky came to a halt and the breathless Kovalyov tore into a small waiting-room where a grey-haired bespectacled clerk in an old frock-coat was sitting at a table with his pen between his teeth, counting out copper coins.

'Who sees to advertisements here?' Kovalyov shouted. 'Ah, good morning.'

'Good morning,' replied the grey-haired clerk, raising his eyes for one second, then looking down again at the little piles of money spread out on the table.

'I want to publish an advertisement.'

'Just one moment, if you don't mind,' the clerk answered, as he wrote down a figure with one hand and moved two beads on his abacus with the other.

A footman who, judging by his gold-braided livery and generally very smart appearance, obviously worked in some noble house, was standing by the table holding a piece of paper and, just to show he could hob-nob with high and low, started rattling away:

'Believe me, that nasty little dog just isn't worth eighty kopecks. I wouldn't give more than sixteen for it. But the Countess dotes on it, and that's why she makes no bones about offering a hundred roubles to the person who finds it. If we're going to be honest with one another, I'll tell you quite openly, there's no accounting for taste. I can understand a fancier paying anything up to five hundred, even a thousand for a deerhound or a poodle, as long as it's a good dog.'

The elderly clerk listened to him solemnly while he carried on totting up the words in the advertisement. The room was crowded with old women, shopkeepers, and houseporters, all holding advertisements. In one of these a coachman of 'sober disposition' was seeking employment; in another a carriage, hardly used, and brought from Paris in 1814, was up for sale; in another a nineteen-year-old servant-girl, with laundry experience, and prepared to do *other* work, was looking for a job. Other advertisements offered a drozhky for sale—in good condition apart from one missing spring; a 'young' and spirited dapple-grey colt seventeen years old; radish and turnip seeds only just arrived from London; a country house, with every modern convenience, including stabling for two horses and enough land for planting an excellent birch or fir forest. And one invited prospective buyers of old boot soles to attend certain auction rooms between the hours of eight and three daily. The room into which all these people were crammed was small and extremely stuffy. But Collegiate Assessor Kovalyov could not smell anything as he had covered his face with a handkerchief—and he could not have smelt anything anyway, as his nose had disappeared God knows where.

'My dear sir, will you take the details down now, *please*. I really can't wait any longer,' he said, beginning to lose patience.

'Just a minute, if you *don't* mind! Two roubles forty-three kopecks. Nearly ready. One rouble sixty-four kopecks,' the grey-haired clerk muttered as he shoved pieces of paper at the old ladies and servants standing around. Finally he turned to Kovalyov and said: 'What do you want?'

'I want . . .' Kovalyov began. 'Something very fishy's been going on, whether it's some nasty practical joke or a plain case of fraud I can't say as yet. All I want you to do is to offer a substantial reward for the first person to find the blackguard . . .'

'Name, please.'

'Why do you need that? I can't tell you. Too many people

know me—Mrs Chekharyev, for example, who's married to a state councillor, Mrs Palageya Podtochin, a staff officer's wife . . . they'd find out who it was at once, God forbid! Just put "Collegiate Assessor", or even better, "Major".'

'And the missing person was a household serf of yours?'

'Household serf? The crime wouldn't be half as serious! It's my *nose* that's disappeared.'

'Hm, strange name. And did this Mr Nose steal much?'

'*My* nose, I'm trying to say. You don't understand! It's my own nose that's disappeared. It's a diabolical practical joke someone's played on me.'

'How did it disappear? I don't follow.'

'I can't tell you how. But please understand, my nose is travelling at this very moment all over the town, calling itself a state councillor. That's why I'm asking you to print this advertisement announcing the first person who catches it should return the nose to its rightful owner as soon as possible. Imagine what it's like being without such a conspicuous part of your body! If it were just a small toe, then I could put my shoe on and no one would be any the wiser. On Thursdays I go to Mrs Chekhtaryev's (she's married to a state councillor) and Mrs Podtochin, who has a staff officer for a husband—and a very pretty little daughter as well. They're all very close friends of mine, so just imagine what it would be like . . . In *my* state how can I visit any of them?'

The clerk's tightly pressed lips showed he was deep in

thought. 'I can't print an advertisement like that in our paper,' he said after a long silence.

'What? Why not?'

'I'll tell you. A paper can get a bad name. If everyone started announcing his nose had run away, I don't know how it would all end. And enough false reports and rumours get past editorial already . . .'

'But why does it strike you as so absurd? *I* certainly don't think so.'

'That's what *you* think. But only last week there was a similar case. A clerk came here with an advertisement, just like you. It cost him two roubles seventy-three kopecks, and all he wanted to advertise was a runaway black poodle. And what do you think he was up to really? In the end we had a libel case on our hands: the poodle was meant as a satire on a government cashier—I can't remember what ministry he came from.'

'But I want to publish an advertisement about my nose, not a poodle, and that's as near myself as dammit!'

'No, I can't accept that kind of advertisement.'

'But I've lost my *nose!*'

'Then you'd better see a doctor about it. I've heard there's a certain kind of specialist who can fix you up with any kind of nose you like. Anyway, you seem a cheery sort, and I can see you like to have your little joke.'

'By all that's holy, I swear I'm telling you the truth. If you really want me to, I'll *show* you what I mean.'

'I shouldn't bother if I were you,' the clerk continued, taking a pinch of snuff. 'However, if it's *really* no trouble,' he added, leaning forward out of curiosity, 'then I shouldn't mind having a quick look.'

The collegiate assessor removed his handkerchief.

'Well, how very peculiar! It's quite flat, just like a freshly cooked pancake. Incredibly flat.'

'So much for your objections! Now you've seen it with your own eyes and you can't possibly refuse. I will be particularly grateful for this little favour, and it's been a real pleasure meeting you.'

The Major, evidently, had decided that flattery might do the trick.

'Of course, it's no problem *printing* the advertisement,' the clerk said. 'But I can't see what you can stand to gain by it. If you like, why not give it to someone with a flair for journalism, then he can write it up as a very rare freak of nature and have it published in *The Northern Bee* (here he took another pinch of snuff) so that young people might benefit from it (here he wiped his nose). Or else, as something of interest to the general public.'

The collegiate assessor's hopes vanished completely. He looked down at the bottom of the page at the theatre guide. The name of a rather pretty actress almost brought a smile to his face, and he reached down to his pocket to see if he had a five-rouble note, since in his opinion staff officers should sit only in the stalls. But then he remembered his nose, and knew he could not possibly think of going to the theatre.

Apparently even the clerk was touched by Kovalyov's terrible predicament and thought it would not hurt to cheer him up with a few words of sympathy.

'Really, I can't say how sorry I am at what's happened. How about a pinch of snuff? It's very good for headaches—and puts fresh heart into you. It even cures piles.'

With these words he offered Kovalyov his snuff-box, deftly flipping back the lid which bore a portrait of some lady in a hat.

This unintentionally thoughtless action made Kovalyov lose patient altogether.

'I don't understand how you can joke at a time like this,' he said angrily. 'Are you so blind you can't see that I've nothing to smell with? You know what you can do with your snuff! I can't bear to look at it, and anyway you might at least offer me some real French rapée, not that filthy Berezinsky brand.'

After this declaration he strode furiously out of the newspaper office and went off to the local Inspector of Police (a fanatical lover of sugar, whose hall and dining room were crammed full of sugar-cubes presented by merchants who wanted to keep well in with him). Kovalyov arrived just when he was having a good stretch, grunting, and saying, 'Now for a nice two hours' nap.' Our collegiate assessor had clearly chosen a very bad time for his visit.

The Inspector was a great patron of the arts and industry, but most of all he loved government banknotes. 'There's nothing finer than banknotes,' he used to say. 'They don't need feeding, take up very little room and slip nicely into the pocket. And they don't break if you drop them.'

The Inspector gave Kovalyov a rather cold welcome and said that after dinner wasn't at all the time to start investigations, that nature herself had decreed a rest after meals (from this our collegiate assessor concluded the Inspector was well versed in the wisdom of antiquity), that *respectable* men do not get their noses ripped off, and that there were no end of majors knocking around who were not too fussy about their underwear who were in the habit of visiting the most disreputable places.

These few home truths stung Kovalyov to the quick. Here I must point out that Kovalyov was an extremely sensitive man. He did not so much mind people making personal remarks about him, but it was a different matter when aspersions were cast on his rank or social standing.

As far as he was concerned they could say what they liked about subalterns on the stage, but staff officers should be exempt from attack.

The reception given him by the Inspector startled him so much that he shook his head, threw out his arms and said in a dignified voice, 'To be frank, after these remarks of yours, which I find very offensive, I have nothing more to say . . .' and walked out. He arrived home hardly able to feel his feet beneath him. It was already getting dark. After his fruitless inquiries his flat seemed extremely dismal and depressing. As he entered the hall he saw his footman Ivan lying on a soiled leather couch spitting at the ceiling, managing to hit the same spot with a fair degree of success. The nonchalance of the man infuriated him and Kovalyov hit him across the forehead with his hat and said: 'You fat pig! Haven't you anything better to do!'

Ivan promptly jumped up and rushed to take off Kovalyov's coat. Tired and depressed, the Major went to his room, threw himself into an armchair and after a few sighs said:

'My God, my God! What have I done to deserve this? If I'd lost an arm or a leg it wouldn't be so bad. Even without any *ears* things wouldn't be very pleasant, but it wouldn't be the end of the world. A man without a nose, though, is God knows what, neither fish nor fowl. Just something to be thrown out of the window. If my nose had been lopped off during the war, or in a duel, at least I might have had some say in the matter. But to lose it for no reason at all and with nothing to show for it, not even a kopeck! No, it's absolutely impossible . . . It can't have gone just like that! Never! Must have been a dream, or perhaps I drank some of that vodka I use for rubbing down my beard after shaving instead of water: that idiot Ivan couldn't have put it back in the cupboard.'

To prove to himself he was not drunk the Major pinched himself so hard that he cried out in pain, which really did convince him he was awake and in full possession of his senses. He stealthily crept over to the mirror and screwed up his eyes in the hope that his nose would reappear in its proper place, but at once he jumped back, exclaiming:

'That ridiculous blank space again!'

It was absolutely incomprehensible. If a button, or a silver spoon, or his watch, or something of that sort had been missing, that would have been understandable. But for his *nose* to disappear from his own flat . . . Major Kovalyov weighed up all the evidence and decided that the most likely explanation of all was that Mrs Podtochin, the staff officer's wife, who wanted to marry off her daughter to him, was to blame, and no one else. In fact he liked chasing after her, but never came to proposing. And when the staff officer's wife used to tell him straight out that she was offering him her daughter's hand, he would politely withdraw, excusing himself on the grounds that he was still a young man, and that he wanted to devote another five years to the service, by which time he would be just forty-two. So, to get her revenge, the staff officer's wife must have hired some witches to spirit it away, and this was the only way his nose could possibly have been cut off—no one had visited him in his flat, his barber Ivan Yakovlevich had shaved him only last Wednesday, and the rest of that day and the whole of Thursday his nose had been intact. All this he remembered quite clearly. Moreover, he would have been in pain and the wound could not have healed as smooth as a pancake in such a short time. He began planning what to do: either he would sue the staff officer's wife for damages, or he would go and see her personally and accuse her point blank.

But he was distracted from these thoughts by the sight of some chinks of light in the door, which meant Ivan had lit a candle in the hall. Soon afterwards Ivan appeared in person, holding the candle in front of him, so that it brightened up the whole room. Kovalyov's first reaction was to seize his handkerchief and cover up the bare place where only yesterday his nose had been, to prevent that stupid idiot from standing there gaping at him. No sooner had Ivan left than a strange voice was heard in the hall:

'Does Collegiate Assessor Kovalyov live here?'

'Please come in. The Major's home,' said Kovalyov, springing to his feet and opening the door.

A smart-looking police officer, with plump cheeks and whiskers that were neither too light nor too dark—the same police officer who had stood on St Isaac's Bridge at the beginning of our story—made his entrance.

'Are you the gentleman who has lost his nose?'

'Yes, that's me.'

'It's been found.'

'What did you say?' cried Major Kovalyov. He could hardly speak for joy. He looked wide-eyed at the police officer, the candle-light flickering on his fat cheeks and thick lips.

'How did you find it?'

'Very strange. We caught it just as it was about to drive off in the Riga stagecoach. Its passport was made out in the name of some civil servant. Strangely enough, I mistook it for a gentleman at first. Fortunately I had my spectacles with me so I could see it was really a nose. I'm very short-sighted, and if you happen to stand just in front of me, I can only make out your face, but not your nose, or beard, or anything else in fact. My mother-in-law (that's to say, on my *wife's* side) suffers from the same complaint.'

Kovalyov was beside himself.

'Where is it? I'll go right away and claim it.'

'Don't excite yourself, sir. I know how much you wanted it back, so I've brought it with me. Very strange, but the main culprit in this little affair seems to be that swindler of a barber from Voznesensky Street: he's down at the station now. I've had my eyes on him a long time on suspicion of drunkenness and larceny, and only three days ago he was found stealing a dozen buttons from a shop. You'll find your nose just as it was when you lost it.'

And the police officer dipped into his pocket and pulled out the nose wrapped up in a piece of paper.

'That's it!' cried Kovalyov, 'no mistake! You *must* stay and have a cup of tea.'

'I'd like to, but I'm expected back at the prison ... The price of food has rocketed ... My mother-in-law (on my *wife's* side) is living with me, and all the children as well; the eldest boy seems very promising, very bright, but we haven't the money to send him to school ...'

Kovalyov guessed what he was after and took a note from the table and pressed it into the officer's hands. The police officer bowed very low and went out into the street, where Kovalyov could hear him telling some stupid peasant who had driven his cart up on the pavement what he thought of him.

When the police officer had gone, our collegiate assessor felt rather bemused and only after a few minutes did he come to his senses at all, so intense was his joy. He carefully took the nose in his cupped hands and once more subjected it to close scrutiny.

'Yes, that's it, that's it!' Major Kovalyov said, 'and there's the pimple that came up yesterday on the left-hand side.' The Major almost laughed with joy.

But nothing is lasting in this world. Even joy begins to fade after only one minute. Two minutes later, and it is weaker still, until finally it is swallowed up in our everyday, prosaic state of mind, just as a ripple made by a pebble gradually merges with the smooth surface of the water. After some thought Kovalyov concluded that all was not right again yet and there still remained the problem of putting the nose back in place.

'What if it doesn't stick?'

With a feeling of inexpressible horror he rushed to the table, and pulled the mirror nearer, as he was afraid that he might stick the nose on crooked. His hands trembled. With great care and caution he pushed it into place. But oh! the nose just would not stick. He warmed it a little by pressing it to his mouth and breathing on it, and then pressed it again to the smooth space between his cheeks. But try as he might the nose would not say on.

'Stay on, you fool!' he said. But the nose seemed to be made of wood and fell on to the table with a strange cork-like sound. The Major's face quivered convulsively. 'Perhaps I can graft it,' he said apprehensively. But no matter how many times he tried to put it back, all his efforts were futile.

He called Ivan and told him to fetch the doctor, who happened to live in the same block, in one of the best flats on the first floor.

This doctor was a handsome man with fine whiskers as black as pitch, and a fresh-looking, healthy wife. Every morning he used to eat apples and was terribly meticulous about keeping his mouth clean, spending at least three quarters of an hour rinsing it out every day and using five different varieties of toothbrush. He came right away. When he had asked the Major if he had had this trouble for very long the doctor pushed back Kovalyov's chin and prodded him with his thumb in the spot once occupied by his nose—so sharply that the Major hit the wall very hard with the back of his head. The doctor told him not to worry and made him stand a little away from the wall and lean his head first to the right. Pinching the place where his nose had been the doctor said 'Hm!' Then he ordered him to move his head to the left and produced another 'Hm!' Finally he prodded him again, making Kovalyov's head twitch like a horse having its teeth inspected.

After this examination the doctor shook his head and said: 'It's no good. It's best to stay as you are, otherwise you'll only make it worse. Of course, it's possible to have it stuck on, and I could do this for you quite easily. But I assure you it would look terrible.'

'That's *marvellous*, that is! How can I carry on without a nose?' said Kovalyov. '*Whatever* you do it couldn't look any worse; and God knows, that's bad enough! How can I go around looking like a freak? I mix with nice people. I'm expected at two soirées today. I know nearly all the best people—Mrs Chekhtaryev, a state councillor's wife, Mrs Podtochin, a staff officer's wife ... after the way *she's* behaved I won't have any more to do with *her*, except when I get the police on her trail.' Kovalyov went on pleading: 'Please do me this one favour—isn't there any way? Even if you only get it to hold on, it wouldn't be so bad, and if there were any risk of it falling off, I could keep it there with my hand. I don't dance, which is a help, because any violent movement might make it drop off. And you may rest assured I wouldn't be slow in showing my appreciation—as far as my pocket will allow of course ...'

The doctor then said in a voice which could not be called loud, or even soft, but persuasive and arresting: 'I never practise my art from purely mercenary motives. That is contrary to my code of conduct and all professional ethics. True,

I make a charge for private visits, but only so as not to offend patients by refusing to take their money. Of course, I could put your nose back if I wanted to. But I give you my word of honour, if you know what's good for you, it would be far worse if I tried. Let nature take its course. Wash the area as much as you can with cold water and believe me you'll feel just as good as when you had a nose. Now, as far as the nose is concerned, put it in a jar of alcohol; better still, soak it in two tablespoonsful of sour vodka and warmed-up vinegar, and you'll get good money for it. I'll take it myself if you don't want it.'

'No! I wouldn't sell it for anything,' Kovalyov cried desperately. 'I'd rather lose it again.'

'Then I'm sorry,' replied the doctor, bowing himself out. 'I wanted to help you . . . at least I've tried hard enough.'

With these words the doctor made a very dignified exit. Kovalyov did not even look at his face, and felt so dazed that all he could make out were the doctor's snowy-white cuffs sticking out from the sleeves of his black dress-coat.

The very next day he decided—before going to the police—to write to the staff officer's wife to ask her to put back in its proper place what belonged to him without further ado. The letter read as follows:

Dear Mrs Alexandra Grigoryevna,

I cannot understand this strange behaviour on your part. You can be sure, though, that it won't get you anywhere and you certainly won't force me to marry your daughter. Moreover, you can rest assured that, regarding my nose, I am familiar with the whole history of this affair from the very beginning, and I also know that you, and no one else, are the prime instigator. Its sudden detachment from its rightful place, its subsequent flight, its masquerading as a civil servant and then its re-appearance in its natural state, are nothing else than the result of black magic carried out by yourself or by those practising the same very honourable art. I consider it my duty to warn you that if the above-mentioned nose is not back in its proper place by today, then I shall be compelled to ask for the law's protection.

I remain, dear Madam,

Your very faithful servant,

Platon Kovalyov.

Dear Mr Kovalyov!

I was simply staggered by your letter. To be honest, I never expected anything of this kind from you, particularly those remarks which are quite uncalled-for. I would have you know I have never received that civil servant mentioned by you in my house, whether disguised or not. True, Philip Ivanovich Potanchikov used to call. Although he wanted to ask for my daughter's hand, and despite the fact that he was a very sober, respectable and learned gentleman, I never gave him any cause for hope. And then you go on to mention your nose. If by this you mean to say I wanted to make you look foolish, that is, to put you off with a formal refusal, then all I can say is that I am very surprised that you can talk like this, as you know well enough my feelings on the matter are quite different. And if you care to make an official proposal to my daughter, I will gladly give my consent, for this has always been my dearest wish, and in this hope I remain at your disposal.

Yours sincerely,
Alexandra Podtochin.

'No,' said Kovalyov when he had read the letter. 'She's not to blame. Impossible! A guilty person could never write a letter like that.' The collegiate assessor knew what he was talking about in this case as he had been sent to the Caucasus several times to carry out legal inquiries. 'How on earth did this happen then? It's impossible to make head or tail of it!' he said, letting his arms drop to his side.

Meanwhile rumours about the strange occurrence had spread throughout the capital, not, need we say, without a few embellishments. At the time everyone seemed very preoccupied with the supernatural: only a short time before, some experiments in magnetism had been all the rage. Besides, the story of the dancing chairs in Konúshenny Street was still fresh in people's minds, so no one was particularly surprised to hear about Collegiate Assessor Kovalyov's nose taking a regular stroll along the Nevsky Avenue at exactly three o'clock every afternoon. Every day crowds of inquisitive people flocked there. Someone said they had seen the nose in Junker's Store and this produced such a crush outside that the police had to be called.

One fairly respectable-looking, bewhiskered character, who sold stale cakes outside the theatre, knocked together some solid-looking wooden benches, and hired them out at eighty kopecks a time for people to stand on.

One retired colonel left home especially early one morning and after a great struggle managed to barge his way through to the front. But to his great annoyance, instead of a nose in the shop window, all he could see was an ordinary woollen jersey and a lithograph showing a girl adjusting her stocking while a dandy with a small beard and cutaway waistcoat peered out at her from behind a tree—a picture which had hung there in that identical spot for more than ten years. He left feeling very cross and was heard to say: 'Misleading the public with such ridiculous and far-fetched stories shouldn't be allowed.'

Afterwards it was rumoured that Major Kovalyov's nose was no longer to be seen strolling along the Nevsky Avenue but was in the habit of walking in Tavrichesky Park, and that it had been doing this for a long time. When Khozrov-Mirza lived there, he was astonished at this freak of nature. Some of the students from the College of Surgeons went to have a look. One well-known, very respectable lady wrote specially to the head park-keeper, asking him to show her children this very rare phenomenon and, if possible, give them an instructive and edifying commentary at the same time.

These events came as a blessing to those socialites (indispensable for any successful party) who loved amusing the ladies and whose stock of stories was completely exhausted at the time.

A few respectable and high-minded citizens were very upset. One indignant gentleman said that he was at a loss to understand how such absurd cock-and-bull stories could gain currency in the present enlightened century, and that the complete indifference shown by the authorities was past comprehension. Clearly this gentleman was the type who likes to make the government responsible for everything, even their daily quarrels with their wives. And afterwards . . . but here again the whole incident becomes enveloped in mist and what happened later remains a complete mystery.

3

This world is full of the most outrageous nonsense. Sometimes things happen which you would hardly think possible: that very same nose, which had paraded itself as a state councillor and created such an uproar in the city, suddenly turned up, as if nothing had happened, plonk where it had been before, i.e. right between Major Kovalyov's two cheeks. This was on 7 April. He woke up and happened to glance at the mirror—there was his nose! He grabbed it with his hand to make sure—but there was no doubt this time. 'Aha!' cried Kovalyov, and if Ivan hadn't come in at that very moment, he would have joyfully danced a trepak round the room in his bare feet.

He ordered some soap and water, and as he washed himself looked into the mirror again: the nose was there. He had another look as he dried himself—yes, the nose was still there!

'Look, Ivan, I think I've got a pimple on my nose.'

Kovalyov thought: 'God, supposing he replies: "Not only is there no pimple, but no nose either!"' But Ivan answered: 'Your nose is quite all right, sir, I can't see any pimple.'

'Thank God for that,' the Major said to himself and clicked his fingers.

At this moment Ivan Yakovlevich the barber poked his head round the corner, but timidly this time, like a cat which had just been beaten for stealing fat.

'Before you start, are your hands clean?' Kovalyov shouted from the other side of the room.

'Perfectly clean.'

'You're lying.'

'On my life, sir, they're clean!'

'Hm, let's have a look then!'

Kovalyov sat down. Ivan Yakovlevich covered him with a

towel and in a twinkling had transformed his whole beard and part of his cheeks into the kind of cream served up at merchants' birthday parties.

'Well, I'll be damned,' Ivan Yakovlevich muttered to himself, staring at the nose. He bent Kovalyov's head to one side and looked at him from a different angle. 'That's *it* all right! You'd never credit it . . .' he continued and contemplated the nose for a long time. Finally, ever so gently, with a delicacy that the reader can best imagine, he lifted two fingers to hold the nose by its tip. This was how Ivan Yakovlevich normally shaved his customers.

'Come on now, and mind my nose!' shouted Kovalyov. Ivan Yakovlevich let his arms fall to his side and stood there more frightened and embarrassed than he had ever been in his life. At last he started tickling Kovalyov carefully under the chin with his razor. And although with only his olfactory organ to hold on to without any other means of support made shaving very awkward, by planting his rough, wrinkled thumb on his cheek and lower gum (in this way gaining some sort of leverage) he managed to shave him.

When everything was ready, Kovalyov rushed to get dressed and took a cab straight to the café. He had hardly got inside before he shouted, 'Waiter, a cup of chocolate,' and went straight up to the mirror. Yes, his nose was there! Gaily he turned around, screwed up his eyes and looked superciliously at two soldiers, one of whom had a nose no bigger than a *waistcoat* button. Then he went off to the ministerial department where he was petitioning for vice-governorship. (Failing this he was going to try for an administrative post.) As he crossed the entrance hall he had another look in the mirror: his nose was still there!

Then he went to see another collegiate assessor (or Major), a great wag whose sly digs Kovalyov used to counter by saying: 'I'm used to your quips by now, you old niggler!'

On the way he thought: 'If the Major doesn't split his sides when he sees me, that's a sure sign everything is in its proper place.' But the collegiate assessor did not pass any remarks. 'That's all right, then, dammit!' thought Kovalyov. In the street he met Mrs Podtochin, the staff officer's wife, who was with her daughter, and they replied to his bow with delighted exclamations: clearly, he had suffered no lasting injury. He had a long chat with them, made a point of taking out his snuff-box, and stood there for ages ostentatiously stuffing both nostrils as he murmured to himself: 'That'll teach you, you old hens! And I'm not going to marry your daughter, simply *par amour*, as they say! If you *don't* mind!'

And from that time onwards Major Kovalyov was able to stroll along the Nevsky Avenue, visit the theatre, in fact go everywhere as though absolutely nothing had happened. And, as though absolutely nothing *had* happened, his nose stayed in the middle of his face and showed no signs of wandering off. After that he was in perpetual high spirits, always smiling, chasing all the pretty girls, and on one occasion even stopping at a small shop in the Gostiny Dvor to buy ribbon for some medal, no one knows why, as he did not belong to any order of knighthood.

And all this took place in the northern capital of our vast empire! Only now, after much reflection, can we see that there is a great deal that is very far-fetched in this story. Apart from the fact that it's *highly* unlikely for a nose to disappear in such a fantastic way and then reappear in various parts of the town dressed as a state councillor, it is hard to believe that Kovalyov was so ignorant as to think newspapers would accept advertisements about noses. I'm not saying I consider such an advertisement too expensive and a waste of money: that's nonsense, and what's more, I don't think I'm a mercenary person. But it's all very nasty, not quite the thing at all, and it makes me feel very awkward! And, come to think of it, how *did* the nose manage to turn up in a loaf of bread, and how *did* Ivan Yakovlevich . . . ? No, I don't understand it, not one bit! But the strangest, most incredible thing of all is that authors should write about such things. That, I confess, is beyond my comprehension. It's just . . . no, no, I don't understand it at all! Firstly, it's no use to the country whatsoever; secondly, it's no use . . . I simply don't know *what* one can make of it . . . However, when all is said and done, one can concede this point or the other and perhaps you can even find . . . well then you won't find much that *isn't* on the absurd side, will you?

And yet, if you stop to think for a moment, there's a grain of truth in it. Whatever you may say, these things do happen—rarely, I admit, but they do happen.

FOR THE BEST IN PAPERBACKS, LOOK FOR THE

In every corner of the world, on every subject under the sun, Penguin represents quality and variety—the very best in publishing today.

For complete information about books available from Penguin—including Puffins, Penguin Classics, and Arkana—and how to order them, write to us at the appropriate address below. Please note that for copyright reasons the selection of books varies from country to country.